Jessi How Long She Had Been Sleeping

when something nudged her awake. She managed to open one eye enough to see the morning light of a stormy dawn and know that it was still raining. Then a strong arm curled around her waist, jolting her into full wakefulness.

A body snuggled up against hers—a naked body that was unmistakably male.

A strange, naked, male body.

In her bed.

* * *

"Ms. Delacorte provides plenty of sparks to please romance fans."

—*Romantic Times Magazine*

Dear Reader,

Welcome to the world of Silhouette Desire, where you can indulge yourself every month with romances that can only be described as passionate, powerful and provocative!

The incomparable Diana Palmer heads the Desire lineup for March. *The Winter Soldier* is a continuation of the author's popular cross-line miniseries, SOLDIERS OF FORTUNE. We're sure you'll enjoy this tale of a jaded hero who offers protection in the form of a marriage of convenience to a beautiful woman in jeopardy.

Bestselling author Leanne Banks offers you March's MAN OF THE MONTH, a tempting *Millionaire Husband,* book two of her seductive miniseries MILLION DOLLAR MEN. The exciting Desire continuity series TEXAS CATTLEMAN'S CLUB: LONE STAR JEWELS continues with *Lone Star Knight* by Cindy Gerard, in which a lady of royal lineage finds love with a rugged Texas cattle baron.

The M.D. Courts His Nurse as Meagan McKinney's miniseries MATCHED IN MONTANA returns to Desire. And a single-dad rancher falls for the sexy horsetrainer he unexpectly hires in Kathie DeNosky's *The Rough and Ready Rancher*. To cap off the month, Shawna Delacorte writes a torrid tale of being *Stormbound with a Tycoon*.

So make some special time for yourself this month, and read all six of these tantalizing Silhouette Desires!

Enjoy!

Joan Marlow Golan

Joan Marlow Golan
Senior Editor, Silhouette Desire

Please address questions and book requests to:
Silhouette Reader Service
U.S.: 3010 Walden Ave., P.O. Box 1325, Buffalo, NY 14269
Canadian: P.O. Box 609, Fort Erie, Ont. L2A 5X3

Stormbound
with a Tycoon
SHAWNA DELACORTE

Published by Silhouette Books
America's Publisher of Contemporary Romance

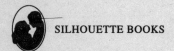 SILHOUETTE BOOKS

ISBN 0-373-76356-5

STORMBOUND WITH A TYCOON

Copyright © 2001 by SKDennison, Inc.

This edition published by arrangement with Harlequin Books S.A.

Visit Silhouette at www.eHarlequin.com

Printed in U.S.A.

Books by Shawna Delacorte

Silhouette Desire

Sarah and the Stranger #730
The Bargain Bachelor #759
Cassie's Last Goodbye #814
Miracle Baby #905
Cowboy Dreaming #1020
Wyoming Wife? #1110
The Tycoon's Son #1157
The Millionaire's Christmas Wish #1187
The Daddy Search #1253
Fortune's Secret Child #1324
Stormbound with a Tycoon #1356

Yours Truly

Much Ado About Marriage

SHAWNA DELACORTE

has delayed her move to Washington State, staying in the Midwest in order to spend some additional time with family. She still travels as often as time permits, and is looking forward to visiting several new places during the upcoming year while continuing to devote herself to writing full-time. Shawna would appreciate hearing from her readers. She can be reached at 6505 E. Central, Box #300, Wichita, KS 67206-1924.

For Thom—*Jeopardy* isn't the same anymore.
We all miss you.

One

Jessica McGuire did not know how long she had been sleeping when something nudged her awake. She managed to open one eye enough to see the morning light of a stormy dawn and know that it was still raining. Then a strong arm curled around her waist, jolting her into full wakefulness. A body snuggled up against hers—a naked body that was unmistakably male.

She froze. A quick rush of fear shot through her. Her heartbeat lodged in her throat. Then an adrenaline surge spurred her into action. She scrambled out of bed and grabbed her oversize T-shirt, hurriedly pulling it on as she started toward the bedroom door. A glance back toward her bed produced a sigh of relief and brought her to a halt. Even though most of his face was hidden from sight, it was obvious that the stranger in her bed was asleep.

Jessica furrowed her brow in confusion, pursed her

lips and cautiously walked over to the side of the bed. She stared at the stranger, trying to get a clear look at his face. Something about him seemed very familiar. She knew him…yet she didn't. Either way, he did not seem to be an immediate threat to her safety.

She tried the light switch. The power was still out, just as it had been last night when she arrived. Power outages were a common occurrence in that part of the Olympic Peninsula whenever a storm swept in from the Pacific Ocean, so the lack of electricity had not been of any concern to her. Besides, she had been just too tired to care as she made her way through the living room of the darkened cabin and climbed the stairs to her bedroom. She had undressed, dropped her clothes on the floor, and collapsed into bed, falling asleep the second her head hit the pillow.

This morning, however, was a different story. She shot a wary glance at the sleeping man in her bed, then turned to pick up the rest of her clothes from the floor. She fully intended to wake this stranger and evict him from her cabin…as soon as she was dressed.

Jessica picked up the last item of clothing and turned to go downstairs to the bathroom as quietly as she could. A gasp caught in her throat as the shock spread through her. The stranger sleeping in her bed was now awake and staring at her. She swallowed hard at the realization that this handsome, sexy man was the naked body that had been snuggled next to her.

The blankets had slipped down to his hips, revealing a strong, athletic build. His dark, tousled hair was matted down on one side where his head had rested against the pillow. Even with the dim, early-morning light she could not miss the mischievous twinkle in his green eyes as he blatantly looked her up and down.

The commotion had forced him awake. He had been in the middle of a tantalizing dream about a warm feminine body nestled next to his with his hand gliding across silky smooth skin. It had all seemed so real and he was not happy about the interruption. He slowly opened his eyes. The sight that greeted him matched his dream in all respects. His gaze started at the floor and climbed up a pair of sleek bare legs to the point where they extended from the bottom of an oversize shirt.

He shifted his attention to the way the shirt clung to her hips and caressed the curves of her breasts. He turned on his side, propped himself up on his elbow and took in the entire woman. She stood about five-six. The disarray of her short blond hair gave her a sexy, wildly uninhibited look. The strong family resemblance told him she was Jessica McGuire...his best friend's sister. She had certainly changed since he last saw her many years ago. This was definitely *not* that awkward teenager.

He made no effort to hide his appreciation of what he was seeing. The thick remnants of sleep gave his voice a husky quality. "Well...well...well...little Jessica McGuire. You've certainly grown up since I last saw you."

"Dylan?" Her mouth fell open as the full shock of his identity hit her. "Dylan Russell? Is that really you?"

"In the flesh." He peeked beneath the blanket that still covered the lower portion of his body, then shot her a decidedly wicked grin. "And I do mean *literally* in the flesh."

The heat of embarrassment spread across Jessica's face. She prided herself on being a self-sufficient, responsible woman who worked hard and maintained a stable life. Waking up to find a naked man in her bed certainly was not part of that life. She attempted to cover her thinly clad body by holding the rest of her clothes in front of her. She wasn't sure, but she thought she detected a chuckle coming from his direction. A jab of irritation poked at her followed by disgust. He certainly didn't seem to have any concerns about his state of undress or the fact that he'd woken up to find a woman in bed with him. It was almost as if he was enjoying her discomfort.

She tried to bring some composure to the moment, but could not quell her annoyance or keep it out of her voice. "You seem to find this situation amusing."

He laughed—the type of sexy laugh that could immediately heat any woman's desires while melting her resolve. "Don't you?"

"No, I don't find it amusing…or charming or *cute*. How did you get here? There wasn't any car outside when I arrived. How did you get in the cabin? The door was locked."

"All questions easily answered." He sat up and ran his fingers through his hair. "You apparently didn't try to put your car in the garage, otherwise you would have seen my car."

"No, I parked as close to the front door as possible so I wouldn't have to run through the rain between the garage and the cabin. But that doesn't explain how you got inside."

"I have a key."

"A key?" As mature, adult and blasé as she tried to be, she couldn't hide her surprise or confusion. "Where did you get a key?"

"Justin gave it to me when he said I could use the cabin for a couple of weeks."

Her tenuous control over the situation began slipping away...assuming she had ever possessed any control over what was happening. Bewilderment replaced confidence as she became less sure of her ground. "Justin offered you the use of our cabin? He didn't say anything to me about it."

An uncomfortable shiver washed across her skin. Dylan seemed to be studying her. He cocked his head and raised an eyebrow. "Maybe that's because he thought you were going to be in New York for three weeks."

"Oh...right." Her voice dropped to a whisper. "New York." He was correct. New York was exactly where she was supposed to be, not at a mountain cabin on the other side of the country. In fact, it was where she had been until the previous morning when she caught a flight back to Seattle after her work project had been postponed.

She pulled her composure together and reasserted her control. "I suggest we put this conversation on hold for a little while. I need to get dressed and you need to get out of my bed...uh, my bed*room*...since it's obvious that you can't continue to stay here."

He eyed her curiously, making no effort to retrieve any clothes. In fact, he snuggled more comfortably into the bed and pulled the blankets up across his chest. "And why not?"

"Why not?" Had she heard him correctly? Was he actually questioning her decision? "I thought that would have been obvious. Because I'm not in New York and you're in *my* bed—that's why not."

"I took the first bedroom I came to."

"This one is mine. The other one is Justin's."

He adopted a businesslike attitude. "You're right. We do need to put this conversation on hold for a while—" he flashed her a teasing grin "—at least until I've had some coffee." He started to lean across the bed and grab his jeans from the arm of the chair, then paused as he glanced in her direction. "Would you mind turning your back so I can put on my pants…or do you prefer to just stand there clutching your clothes in front of you?"

"It's *my* bedroom…you're the one who should…I mean…" She saw the expression dart across his face, the one that said he was about to pull back the covers and get out of bed. "I didn't mean—"

The heat of embarrassment burned across her cheeks. She whirled around and hurried out the door, her clothes clutched tightly against her body. The amused chuckle followed her down the stairs and into the bathroom. She closed out the sound by shutting the bathroom door.

Jessica pulled back the shower curtain, sat on the edge of the bathtub and closed her eyes. She did not know whether to be angry at his intrusion or amused by his audacity. Her annoyance surfaced. He had certainly gone out of his way to embarrass her. And this wasn't the first time, either. Her thoughts drifted back to the time when she was sixteen years old.

Justin had brought Dylan home with him during a school break. Unlike the previous year when the awkward fifteen-year-old Jessica had developed a huge crush on Dylan and had tried all weekend without success to get his attention, the sixteen-year-old Jessica had basked in his attentiveness. Dylan had played cards with her, talked to her and then asked her if she

wanted to go out to lunch. He had even bought her a
stuffed bear to add to her collection. Obviously, he
liked her very much, hopefully as much as she liked
him.

She had dressed in her most sophisticated outfit, put
on extra makeup and did her hair up on top of her
head, all to show him she was mature enough to date
a twenty-year-old college man. But when it came time
for lunch, she had been devastated to find that it was
not the date she'd thought it would be. It was a group
lunch of nearly a dozen people and she was the only
one who had dressed up. The worst part was that Dylan had brought a date with him.

She had been humiliated and embarrassed. She had
never forgotten the incident, even though, in retrospect, she realized he had done nothing to lead her on
and was only being polite in trying to include her with
the group. She had heard what she'd wanted to hear
rather than what Dylan had actually said or meant, but
it had still been an emotionally traumatic incident that
she had never forgotten.

But that was ancient history. She was now a mature,
intelligent woman of thirty-one, not the type to be easily swayed by a handsome man with thick, dark hair,
emerald-green eyes, a dazzling smile…and danger
written all over him.

She pursed her lips and wrinkled her brow into a
slight scowl. From what her brother had told her of
Dylan Russell's lifestyle, finding a woman in his bed
was certainly not an unusual occurrence. Her scowl
turned to contemplation. What was Dylan Russell doing there? He was not the type of man who would
hide away in an isolated mountain cabin and certainly
not without the benefit of feminine companionship.

Everything she had ever heard about him said he was a charming rogue, a personable scoundrel who drifted from one quick-buck deal to another and one bed to another, without any roots, commitments or responsibilities.

Her contemplation turned to confusion. He was a globe-trotting playboy who would surely feel more comfortable in a luxury resort with a hot tub and room service. So what was he doing by himself in her cabin? Then another thought struck her. Could he be expecting someone to meet him there? A woman? The quick jab of anger caught her by surprise. She immediately shoved it away. His personal life was none of her business.

Even though she had always found her brother's stories about Dylan to be fascinating, she knew no good would come from pursuing an interest in that sort of man regardless of how sexy and exciting she found him. And Dylan Russell certainly ranked at the top of any list of sexy and exciting men. She knew from experience that his type was all outward flash without any real substance underneath. She had been married to a handsome man with a roving eye and little concern about whose bed he frequented. She had no desire to travel down that path again. She dismissed the errant thoughts. Right now she needed to get dressed.

Jessica was not the only one contemplating the events of the past few minutes.

Dylan stared out the bedroom door toward the steps leading down to the living room. His teasing banter with Jessica had turned out to be far more interesting than he would have imagined. In fact, Jessica was far more interesting than he would have imagined. Justin painted his sister as an organized, no-nonsense type of person who knew what she wanted out of life and had her feet firmly planted on the ground—certainly not the type of woman he was accustomed to dating. What Justin failed to mention was that his sister was also drop-dead gorgeous with a body that would not quit.

Exactly where had Jessica McGuire been three months ago when he needed someone just like her? When everything turned sour and his life started falling apart? He shook his head and reminded himself that she was his best friend's sister. He was not sure exactly what that meant, but the cautionary thought popped into his head. He could not consider this beautiful, intelligent woman who knew who she was and where she was going in life as another potential bedmate.

Dylan took a deep breath, then slowly expelled it. He tried to clear his mind of the wayward thoughts, but he could not clear away the memory of her body snuggled next to his and his hand sliding across her silky skin. Nor could he erase the sight of her standing next to the bed, her mussed hair and scantily clad body giving her a look of sexy, uninhibited abandon. A tightness pulled across his chest. He took another deep breath in hopes of breaking the restrictive feeling, then threw back the covers, climbed out of bed, dressed and headed toward the stairs.

Dylan stopped short at the bottom step. He could see Jessica through the kitchen door. A scowl marred her otherwise beautiful face. She seemed to be staring at something. He entered the kitchen, walked up behind her and peered over her shoulder in an attempt to see what had captured her attention and caused her to frown like that.

"Is something wrong?"

The sound of his voice startled her. She jerked around and found her face almost touching his. For a long moment she looked up into the intensity of his green eyes, or more accurately, he seemed to be pulling her into the depth of those eyes as he searched her face for some sort of explanation.

"Uh—" she took a couple of steps away from his uncomfortable nearness "—wrong?"

"You were scowling at the stove. Is there something wrong?"

She took yet another step farther away from his disconcerting presence, coming to a halt when she bumped into the kitchen counter. Her voice held the same uncertainty that coursed through her veins. "Wrong?" She knew she sounded like an idiot, parroting the same word over and over. She gathered her composure and projected as much confidence as she could muster, but she couldn't quell the disturbing sensations playing havoc in her stomach.

"There isn't any gas...the stove burner won't light, there's no hot water and the floor furnace in the living room won't light. There must be something wrong with the propane tank."

"I didn't use any hot water and didn't even try to turn on the furnace or the stove when I arrived last night. I went right to bed. I was going to read for a while, but then the storm knocked the electricity out."

"The tank shouldn't have been turned off. It was just filled a week ago and was supposed to have been left on." She glanced toward the window, then looked up at the ceiling and the sound of the rain pounding against the roof.

An exasperated sigh accompanied her words.

"Damn…there doesn't seem to be any way to avoid going out into the rain to see what's wrong."

"Where is the propane tank?"

"It's behind the garage."

Dylan glanced out the window. "It's raining pretty hard. I'll go out and check it. You stay inside where it's dry."

"Forget it." She snapped out the words. "I'm capable of taking care of it myself."

"Whoa…" A slight edge of irritation crept into his voice. "I didn't say you weren't capable. I merely offered to help."

Jessica grabbed a jacket from the coatrack by the front door. "You weren't offering to help, you were *telling* me what to do." She shoved her arms into the sleeves, turned up the collar, then opened the front door.

She paused long enough to shoot a contemptuous look in his direction. "I don't need your help." Then she stepped out onto the porch prepared to brave the elements.

She bit at her lower lip in a moment of contemplation. Perhaps she had been a little harsh with her comments. He really hadn't said anything wrong. She clenched her jaw in determination. Dylan Russell had totally unnerved her and she didn't like it. She hunched her shoulders against the chilly air and ran out into the rain.

Dylan stared after her, his annoyance overriding her show of irritation. She had literally dismissed him as if he had made some sort of disparaging comment rather than a sincere offer of help. He was not accustomed to being treated in that manner, especially by a beautiful woman. He allowed a brief instant of reflection. Of course, he wasn't accustomed to dealing with independent, self-sufficient women who would even know what a propane tank was let alone what to do with one.

He followed her out into the rain, catching up with her just as she rounded the corner of the garage. He stood by as she bent down and checked the gauge on the tank, then made sure the connection was tight. She glanced up at him, raising her hand to shield her eyes from the rain. "The valve's closed. The tank has been shut off."

She opened the valve to start the flow of propane to the cabin, then she straightened up and took a couple of steps forward until he blocked her way. They stood very close together, almost as close as when they had been in the kitchen.

The tightness spread across his chest again as he stared at her. The rain matted her hair against her head. Rivulets of water ran down her face and formed her long, dark eyelashes into spiky clumps. He started to reach out and touch her, but managed to resist the urge. He wanted to wipe the water from her cheek and kiss away the droplets from her all-too-tempting lips. It was the kind of delicious-looking mouth that would drive any man to distraction. He forced down the desire and reluctantly stepped aside.

She remained rooted to the spot, unable to move. Every fiber of her being screamed out for the physical contact that was almost there but not quite. She swallowed down the lump lodged in her throat and tried to still her racing pulse. She finally managed, with difficulty, to break away from the invisible hook pulling her into the realm of his masculinity. She broke into a run, quickly covering the ground back to the cabin.

He followed closely behind. When they reached the covered porch she removed her rain-soaked jacket and shook off the excess water, then pulled off her muddy boots and left them on the porch before going inside. Dylan followed suit by kicking off his shoes, too. Once inside she hung her jacket on the coatrack to dry.

He pulled his wet sweatshirt off over his head, revealing a wet T-shirt. She tried not to stare at the way it clung to the well-defined planes of his hard body, but her attempts were useless. Her breathing quickened and, much to her dismay, her pulse started to race again. Somehow she had to put a stop to the physical effect he had on her.

He hooked the sweatshirt over the doorknob, then ran his fingers through his wet hair before turning toward her. "I guess that answers the question about the heat and hot water. Where do you keep the matches?" He glanced around the large open expanse of the cabin's living room and dining room, then toward the kitchen door. "In the kitchen?"

She forced a calm to the inner turmoil running rampant through her body, at least enough to hopefully fool him with a neutral outer manner. "The propane company must have turned the tank off when they filled it last week, then forgot to turn it back on."

She retrieved the matches from the fireplace mantel. "It's lucky for you I showed up when I did to fix things." Her thoughts had slipped out without her meaning to say them aloud.

He bristled at her words. "Turning on a propane

tank and putting a match to some pilot lights is not beyond my capabilities.''

The heat of embarrassment spread across her cheeks. What was wrong with her? She didn't seem to be able to stop herself from taking a cheap shot at him. "I didn't mean to imply—''

A sharp edge of sarcasm surrounded his words. "Since you obviously have everything well under control, I'll leave the work to you to finish. I'll take this opportunity to get out of these wet clothes. If you'll excuse me—'' He turned and walked away from her.

Jessica watched as he climbed the steps. This man that she remembered as being larger than life had suddenly been reduced in stature to that of the ordinary guy next door wearing wet clothes and dripping water on the floor. Well, perhaps ordinary was not the correct word. There was nothing ordinary about Dylan Russell, nor about the surprisingly unsettled effect he had on her. As if to reinforce her thoughts and feelings, a little tremor darted through her body letting her know she was not as in control as she hoped.

Dylan stripped off his wet clothes. He was not sure exactly what to think about the unexpected turn of events that had filled the morning. He didn't have any experience with women who were anything more than a stunning decoration on his arm and a very enthusiastic partner in his bed.

But that was no longer the case for him. It had been quite a while since he was last intimately involved with any type of woman. It certainly had not been for lack of opportunity. The thrill of the chase no longer excited him, especially when the quarry offered no challenge. Jessica certainly did not fit into that mold. He was not sure exactly what mold she did fit into, but he strongly suspected it was not any type familiar to him.

He took a pair of warm socks, a sweater and jeans from the dresser where he'd placed his clothes the night before when he unpacked. As he dressed, his thoughts continued to center around Jessica. He found her beautiful, intelligent, intriguing…and very disconcerting.

He recalled her comment about it being lucky for him that she was there to fix things at the cabin. He did not like her implication that he was incapable of having taken care of those simple tasks. Was that the image he projected? The opinion people held of him? Someone who basically drifted along without purpose or plan? Someone who wasn't capable of handling the simple little tasks of day-to-day life? He clenched his jaw into a tight line. He did not like it, but knew it was what they believed.

It was a realization he had come to three months ago when a business deal had gone bad, throwing him into a downward spiral of depression. It wasn't the business deal itself and certainly not the loss of profits that had so strongly affected him. It was much more than that. It was the reason he had asked Justin for the use of the cabin. He had choices to consider and decisions to make. He had to do something about straightening out his life.

He glanced toward the stairs leading down to the living room. And just how was he going to be able to accomplish anything with the unexpected distraction of the very desirable Jessica McGuire?

Coffee…he needed some hot coffee to take away the damp chill. He started toward the stairs, then turned back. There was no reason to intrude on her privacy by continuing to use her bedroom. Nothing would be gained by purposely antagonizing her. He quickly moved his belongings to the other bedroom.

As soon as he finished, he hurried downstairs. He had brought a few groceries with him, but not enough to accommodate two people for more than a couple of days. When the rain let up, one of them would have to go to the little market on the main road. The reality of his thoughts stopped him cold in his tracks. Somewhere along the line he had apparently decided that the two of them would share the cabin, or, more specifically, that he did not intend to leave.

Even while moving his clothes to the other bedroom the thought had not crystallized in that manner. He squelched the mischievous grin that tried to take hold. Just how was the *in charge* Jessica going to handle that idea? His amusement was short-lived. As soon as he reached the living room he saw the unhappy look on her face.

"If you're through with *my* bedroom, I'd like to change into some dry clothes."

"Certainly." He stepped aside, still not sure where her testy attitude had come from or why. He decided to let her discover for herself that he had moved his things out of her bedroom.

She started up the stairs, paused, then turned back toward him just long enough to level a disagreeable look in his direction. It appeared as if she were about to say something, then changed her mind and continued up the stairs.

He was not sure exactly what the look conveyed, but it made him uncomfortable. It was more than her merely being unhappy with his presence. There was something else in her look, and he couldn't quite place it. They had met on a couple of occasions many years ago, but that did not change the fact that as adults they were virtually strangers to each other. He knew it was an awkward situation and he wasn't at all sure exactly how to resolve it so that they each had what they wanted…or in his case, what he *needed*.

And what he desperately needed was this escape to solitude. He did not want to deal with the ongoing bustling activity of a resort, the impersonal nature of a hotel or the closed-in feeling of being confined to a room as the only way to avoid crowds and activity. Justin's cabin had been the perfect solution to his needs—isolation without feeling closed in.

The A-frame cabin had a large, open expanse consisting of a living room and dining area. The main level also contained a kitchen and a bathroom. Upstairs was a loft overlooking part of the living room, two bedrooms and a deck that stretched all the way across the front of the cabin above the porch. The cabin was big enough that it wasn't confining and was surrounded by forest where he could hike without running into other people.

His entire life seemed to be in turmoil, and he was not sure what to do about it. He needed to think things out, to make some decisions…and to do it quickly before things became worse. His thoughts turned to Stanley and Rose Clarkson. He shoved away the horrible guilt that welled inside him whenever he thought of them.

Coffee…he needed some coffee. He headed for the kitchen. The electric coffeemaker on the counter was useless without any electricity. He shuffled through the kitchen cabinets in search of an old percolator to use on the stove. He finally got down on his hands and knees to look in the back of the lower cupboards.

Jessica came downstairs after changing clothes. She paused at the kitchen door and watched him as he rummaged around looking for something. His jeans fit his legs and across his rear end like a second skin. Even with his loose sweater, she could still discern his muscular back and broad shoulders. She closed her eyes, but it didn't help. She couldn't keep out the vision from early that morning—Dylan propped up on his elbow with the blanket down around his hips, the well-defined planes of his hard chest clearly visible in the early-morning light, the impish grin on his handsome face and the devilish twinkle in his eyes.

She shook away the unwelcome image and tried to settle the butterflies in her stomach. She forced a calm tone to her words that was far removed from what she felt. "What are you looking for?"

He jerked his head up at the sound of her voice and promptly banged it on the edge of the countertop. He scrunched up his face in pain as he rubbed his hand across the sore spot. Jessica suppressed an amused chuckle, although it wasn't easy. This certainly was not the time or the place for laughter.

A moment later he withdrew his other hand from the cabinet, his fingers wrapped firmly around the handle of the old coffeepot. He held his prize out toward her, the triumphant grin covering his face. "I was looking for this."

She flipped the light switch on and off again, somehow needing to personally confirm that the electricity was still out. "Well...I'm glad you found it. Coffee was the foremost thing on my mind, too." The foremost thing if she discounted the very appealing image of Dylan Russell in her bed.

Two

Dylan stood up, set the coffeepot on the counter and flashed his most engaging smile. "I'm glad we found something we could agree on. Now, where do you keep the coffee?"

"I'll do that. I know where everything is." Jessica opened the door of the small pantry and removed the canister.

He took it from her, his tone showing a hint of irritation at her continued derogatory attitude about his capabilities. "I know how to make coffee." He added water to the pot, measured the coffee and lit the burner on the stove. He took two coffee mugs from the cupboard and set them on the kitchen counter. Then he stared intently at the coffeepot as if willing it to start perking.

She turned toward the bathroom. "The water heater

should have done its job and produced some hot water by now. I'm going to take a shower."

"Sure…" He glanced in her direction. "I'll grab a quick shower when you've finished." He ran his hand over the stubble that covered his chin and cheeks. "I need to shave, too." He saw the expression on her face again, the one that said she wanted to say something but had decided against it. He returned his attention to the coffeepot, hoping she would accept that as a sign to go about her business. A couple of minutes later he heard the shower.

Dylan leaned against the kitchen counter and expelled a sigh of relief that she had gone. Other than a couple of delightful minutes when he first woke up, the entire morning had been uncomfortable and very awkward. He had turned on the old charm, but she had refused to succumb.

Jessica McGuire was obviously a very capable woman. He had no experience with women like that—smart, capable, unpretentious and down to earth. He could not imagine even one of the women he had dated over the years actually running out into the rain and mud to check on a propane tank, let alone knowing what to do with it when she got there. He had racked up lots of exciting days and memorable nights, but during the past three months he had been forced to admit, if only to himself, that in spite of everything it had been a lonely existence. It was a bitter pill to swallow and one that had not gone down easily, but he knew it was the truth.

A hard stab of despair hit him when the memory of what happened to Stanley and Rose Clarkson popped into his mind again. Where it had always been a game for him in the past, it had finally dawned on him that he was now thirty-five years old and did not have anything important to show for his life. He had lots of memorable adventures, thousands of acquaintances around the world and a net worth of several million dollars, but he didn't have a real home, a family or any really close friends other than Justin McGuire. He didn't have the things that truly mattered.

Jessica was so different from any other woman he had ever known. She did not hang on his every word, laugh at his jokes whether they were funny or not, jump to fulfill his every whim. In short, she made no effort to impress him or play up to his ego, and he was not sure exactly how to handle it. In time gone past he wouldn't have given it any more thought. He would have simply moved on to someone more receptive. But now...well, she had him confused. He was sure of one thing, though. He had to do something to counter her obviously negative opinion of him. But what?

As soon as the coffee was ready he poured himself a mug and took it into the living room. He opened the front door and stared out at the rain. The cold, damp air chilled him in spite of the coffee that heated the inside of his mouth and his throat. He had to find something he could do that would show Jessica he was not as out of place at the cabin or as inept as she seemed to think. Then his gaze fell on the firewood stacked neatly on the porch.

He glanced back at the cold fireplace. That was it. There was nothing like a warm, cozy fire to break the ice. He returned his coffee mug to the kitchen counter, then set to work carrying in firewood and building a fire. He definitely knew about using a cozy fire to create a romantic mood. Or, in this case, at least a friendly mood that was devoid of the prevailing tension.

He could not stop the little grin that tugged at the corners of his mouth. They could pull chairs up close to the fire and drink their morning coffee in a setting conducive to conversation. He would be able to change her abject opinion of him. Yes, indeed. He was very pleased with himself and his plan.

When he had finished with the fireplace he went to the kitchen to retrieve his coffee mug. He called to Jessica when he heard her emerge from the bathroom. "Coffee's ready. Do you take anything in it or is black okay?" He stood poised with the pot in his hand waiting for her answer.

"Oh, my God! What have you done?" Jessica's cry of alarm filled the air as much as the smell of smoke that quickly replaced the aroma of fresh coffee. It billowed out of the fireplace and into the living room. Her first thought said the cabin was on fire, but before she could act on that assumption she realized it was something else.

Dylan charged across the room toward the fireplace while shouting instructions. "Open the front door and a couple of windows to draw the smoke out." He snatched the largest logs that had not yet caught fire and dropped them on the hearth. He used the poker and scattered the burning kindling around the fireplace to break up the fire's fuel. Then he grabbed the bucket of sand he had spotted on the front porch and spread it over what was left of the fire to smother it.

Jessica stepped out to the front porch and took a deep breath of the crisp fresh air. She was not sure exactly what to think. It was obvious to her that he had stupidly left the damper in the chimney closed—

too much high living and not enough practical experience with real life. She furrowed her brow in thought as another realization hit her. He had also taken immediate charge of the emergency and handled it with calm efficiency.

She set her jaw into a firm line and shook her head to clear her mind of the unwanted, compromising thought. After all, she had every right to be angry with him for enveloping her cabin in smoke and causing a potential disaster. She stubbornly refused to allow any contradictory thoughts to cloud the issue. She stepped back inside the living room, paused for a moment, then made her way over to the fireplace where Dylan had busied himself cleaning up the mess.

The morning had been filled with more than enough tension, and she was not sure exactly what to think or feel about the events that had already transpired. She knew she had been a little harsh, and possibly even unfair, but she didn't seem to be able to stop herself. It was as if some sort of self-defense mechanism had automatically kicked in to protect her from the charms of this handsome and far-too-sexy scoundrel.

She tried to prevent any irritation from creeping into her voice. ''Apparently you failed to open the damper before starting the fire.''

He straightened and leveled an appraising look at her. Was she challenging him? Accusing him? He did not know how to read her. ''I've lit more than my share of fires in various fireplaces. I can assure you that I know enough to check. The damper was open.'' With that, he turned toward the kitchen and the coffee he had left there.

He glanced back at the fireplace just in time to see her kneel down in front of the hearth and reach for the lever that controlled the damper. A little flicker of satisfaction settled inside him as the sheepish expression covered her face when she looked up and saw him watching her. She brushed her hands against her jeans, then slowly walked across the living room to the kitchen.

Dylan cocked his head and arched an eyebrow. "Well?" He saw the crimson tinge of embarrassment spread across her cheeks. She glanced at the floor before regaining eye contact with him.

"You...uh...you were right. The damper is open. I...uh...well, apparently there's something else blocking the chimney."

His sharply clipped words carried an edge of sarcasm. "That's a safe guess."

He continued to stare at her, waiting for her to make the next move. She had accused him of not knowing enough to check the damper and doubted his word when he told her it was open, even to the point of checking it for herself. She had no option other than admitting that he had not been responsible for the fiasco.

The entire morning he had been on the receiving end of her disapproval and skepticism. Now that he had finally gained the upper hand over the circumstances, he wasn't sure he wanted to let her off the hook quite so easily. Things were finally starting to feel a little more comfortable and familiar. He suppressed a grin and settled into the *game*. It was an interesting situation packed with lots of possibilities. So why was he still feeling a little uneasy...and a lot unsure?

He tried to maintain a stern expression, but it wasn't easy. Even though his feelings about her were very confused, they certainly were not hostile. He took a quick inventory of the physical attributes of this very enticing woman. A band tightened across his chest, and the heat of desire churned deep inside him. His feelings were definitely not hostile...quite the contrary.

She squirmed uncomfortably for a moment, then visibly pulled her composure together. She squared her shoulders and aimed an unflinching stare at him. "You're not going to make this easy for me, are you?"

He purposely widened his eyes in feigned innocence. "Make what easy for you?" Justin had told him about his sister hating to admit being wrong, that she was very stubborn in that regard. For reasons he could not clearly define, he was enjoying her being on the spot for a change rather than him. It was an interesting moment of pointed banter with the delightful Jessica McGuire.

She took in a calming breath, then loudly expelled it. An edge of irritation clung to her words. "All right!" She took another calming breath. "You were right and I was wrong. The damper was open." She glared at him with as much of a challenge in her eyes as in her voice. "There—are you satisfied now?"

He flashed her a dazzling smile, freely allowing the sound of victory to fill his voice. "That wasn't really so difficult, was it?"

"Yes, it was!" Her angry retort quickly turned to an awkward moment as she shifted her weight from one foot to the other. She rubbed her hand across the back of her neck and glanced at the floor. Her words were soft, her voice a whisper. "I just assumed—"

"You assumed...what? That I'm a hopelessly inept

jerk who isn't capable of handling the most basic task?'' He saw the embarrassment color her cheeks again and he immediately regretted the harshness of his words, regardless of how true they had been.

She tried to recover the upper hand. ''You have to admit that your lifestyle certainly doesn't lend itself to—''

''Perhaps my 'lifestyle' isn't what you think it is.'' He clenched his jaw in an attempt to bite off his anger. ''True, I've spent the past few years more or less wandering around...'' The sadness and despair that suddenly welled inside him forced an end to his comments.

He turned the word over in his mind. *Lifestyle.* He had no purpose in life or even any goals. Always a party to go to, but no one special with whom to share the joys or the sorrows...especially the sorrows. That was not a lifestyle—it was loneliness.

He had always envied Justin, who seemed to have everything he didn't. Even though Justin was divorced, he had family and was very close to his sister. He had a career he loved, a home and close friends. He had roots, something that was important to him. And Jessica—she was a very together lady. They had everything that mattered. They had what he very much wanted.

What little family Dylan started with had long ago been taken away. He was an only child. His father had deserted the family when he was ten years old. He eventually learned that his father had died five years later. His mother died within two weeks of the time he had been left literally at the altar on his wedding day. It seemed that those closest to him had deserted him. It was a lesson he had learned the hard way—if you allow someone into your heart or to touch your place of vulnerability you will end up being hurt. Close emotional attachments weren't for him, but he truly envied Justin and Jessica.

Dylan turned away before his moment of melancholy became obvious to Jessica. It was just the type of vulnerability he did not want to show to this woman who had already developed some very definite opinions of him. He grabbed the empty coffee mug from the kitchen counter, filled it and handed it to her. He forced an upbeat attitude to his tone. "You never answered me about cream or sugar."

"Just black." She reached out to take the mug from his hand. Their fingers touched for an instant, the warmth much more than what was being generated by the coffee. Her gaze locked with his, held there as if by some force beyond her control. Her breath froze in her lungs. She finally managed to look away, but it did not still the pounding of her heart.

He carried his coffee mug to the living room, taking a swallow as he walked. He desperately wanted to smooth out the tension that permeated the air. Then an incident from his youth popped into his mind. He couldn't stop the chuckle that accompanied it.

She stared at him, her expression part curiosity and part irritation. "This entire morning has been a disaster. Just what is it that you find so funny?"

He took another sip of his coffee and settled into a comfortable chair. "The disaster with the fireplace reminded me of something that happened a long time ago, when I was about fifteen years old." Another soft chuckle escaped his throat as the recollection from his past settled over him.

"My mother and I lived in an old house that had a

fireplace left over from a time before the furnace had been installed. She was down the block playing cards with the neighbors. I decided it was a perfect evening to invite my girlfriend over on the pretext of our studying together. I planned to build this romantic fire in the fireplace the way I'd seen in movies.''

"At fifteen years old you were planning romantic evenings?"

He shot her a sly sidelong glance. "Fifteen-year-old hormones are difficult to argue with." He allowed a quiet moment of reflection as the memory of simpler times warmed his consciousness.

"I had wood, newspapers and matches, all the things I thought I needed to build this romantic fire. I had everything put together the way I thought it should be, with newspaper on the bottom, little pieces of wood on top of that, then bigger pieces on the top of the pile. It was time for her to arrive. I struck a match and lit the newspaper which immediately flared up and caught the small pieces of wood. When I was sure the fire was going I opened the front door and went out on the porch to watch for her. Before I knew what was happening, the room filled with smoke and it billowed out the door. A neighbor saw the smoke and called the fire department.''

He turned and looked at her. "And that's how I learned about dampers in a fireplace." He emitted another gentle laugh mixed with a hint of embarrassment. "What about you? Do you have any *most embarrassing moment* from your past that you'd like to share?"

Only two truly embarrassing moments leaped to her mind. The first one was having several people show up for what she thought was her lunch date with Dylan when she was sixteen years old. The other was catching her husband in bed with another woman. She had no intention of mentioning either incident. "I...uh...can't think of anything right now."

"Oh, I see. I'm left here with my embarrassment exposed, and you're keeping yours a secret." His teasing grin let her know he wasn't angry or upset.

He had shared a personal experience with her, something from his past. It was a warm few minutes that left her enveloped in a feeling of closeness, one totally different from anything she had been prepared for. It was as if she was seeing a totally different Dylan Russell than the one she assumed she knew. The reflective moment was broken when he rose from the chair.

"I guess the next order of business is to figure out exactly what's blocking the chimney." He bent down on the hearth and attempted to look up into the darkness, then turned back toward her. "Do you have a flashlight somewhere around here?"

"Yes, in the kitchen. I'll get it for you." She hurried to the kitchen. Her desire to escape the smooth presence that had been lulling her into a very receptive mood was as strong as the need to retrieve the flashlight. She quelled the uncertainty churning in her stomach. Nothing was as it should be—least of all Dylan Russell. It was more than Justin having let him use the cabin. More than her having inadvertently climbed into bed with him. She feared just how much more it might turn out to be.

Every time she tried to force him into a predetermined mold of who and what he was, he refused to fit. The harder she pushed and shoved, the more he seemed to resist. She found it very perplexing and very frustrating. She had a knack for being able to tag people as to who and what they were, but he refused to cooperate. Every time he flashed that sexy smile she increased her efforts to put him in his place and he seemed to resist all that much harder.

She toyed with the idea that she wanted him neatly classified because she felt threatened by his devil-may-care freedom to do as he pleased whenever it pleased him. It angered her that without even seeming to try, he had managed to make a mockery of her ordered and sensible life. But that wasn't the worst of it.

His nearness sent little tremors of excitement racing through her body...tremors over which she had no control. And all this just from his presence. Other than when he wrapped his arm around her waist while he was asleep, there had been no physical contact between them. Unless you counted the brief moment when their fingers touched—a moment she could still feel as if it had happened only a second ago.

He was not a physical threat, but he surely was a very real emotional one. She reminded herself that she was no longer that impressionable fifteen-year-old schoolgirl who had the major crush on her older brother's friend. Nor was she the sixteen-year-old whose heart had been broken by the very same Dylan Russell. She swept the inappropriate thoughts from her mind and went in search of the flashlight and spare batteries.

Dylan shuffled through a couple of closets while Jessica looked for the flashlight. He found a broom, an old mop handle and some duct tape. By overlapping the ends of the handles and taping them together, he had ended up with a long pole.

"What's that supposed to be?" Jessica asked as she handed him the flashlight.

He leaned the pole against the wall and took the flashlight from her. "I'm making something long enough to reach up the chimney so I can dislodge whatever it is without having to go up on the roof and tackle it from that direction."

"Go up on the roof?" Surely he wasn't serious about actually doing it. "It's still raining. The roof has a very steep slope. It's much too dangerous."

"I know." He cupped her chin in his hand and uttered the words slowly, as if talking to a child. "That's why I don't want to go up on the roof if it can be avoided." He saw the irritation dart across her face and immediately flashed a grin to let her know he was teasing.

Then his gaze found hers. His fingers brushed across her cheek. It was a fleeting moment of intimacy that nearly took his breath away and left him totally confused. He tried to ignore the rush of heated desire by returning to the problem with the chimney.

He snapped on the flashlight, leaned on the hearth and stuck his head into the fireplace. He sighted along the beam of light as it penetrated the darkness. "There's something there, all right. It looks like it's pretty far up. I hope this makeshift pole can reach it."

He withdrew from the fireplace and handed her the flashlight. "Here. Shine the light up there while I try to dislodge the obstruction."

Jessica leaned into the fireplace and turned on the flashlight, shining the beam up into the darkness. Dylan stared at her for a moment, then broke out in a soft chuckle. "You might want to get your head out of there unless you want whatever comes down the chimney to fall in your face.''

She scooted out of the way while muttering under her breath, ''I knew that.''

He teased her obvious irritation at her own mistake. ''Uh...what was that? I didn't hear what you said.''

She angrily snapped out a response to his teasing. ''Are we going to try to clear out this chimney or not?''

''Oh, yes, ma'am. That's exactly what we're going to do.'' Again, he could not contain his amusement.

He turned his attention to the business at hand. He kept as far away from the chimney opening as he could, yet still be in a position to see what he was doing. It was not an ideal situation, but he was willing to give it a try. He shoved the pole as far up into the chimney as he could, finally making contact with whatever had the opening blocked. He jabbed at it. Bits of dried twigs and leaves began to drift down, then suddenly everything gave way.

The accumulated debris broke loose and crashed down the flue into the interior of the fireplace. Jessica jumped to her feet, dropping the flashlight as she tried to keep the flying dust out of her eyes. Dylan choked back a cough as he escaped the cloud of soot and ashes that billowed across the hearth.

They dashed out to the front porch to escape the choking air inside the cabin. Jessica ruffled her fingers through her hair to dislodge some leaves, then brushed her hands across her forehead and cheeks to wipe away the dust. ''What a mess.''

''I think we got the blockage cleared out.'' Dylan picked the bits of twigs from his clothes. ''Do you have a vacuum cleaner? That powdery, fine, fireplace ash is going to be hard to get with a broom.''

''Yes, but there's no—''

''No electricity!'' Dylan finished her sentence.

Each broke out into a spontaneous laugh at the totally ludicrous situation. Almost as quickly as it began the laughter faded when their gazes locked again for a moment…a very heated moment. It was almost an involuntary gesture on Dylan's part as he reached out and gently brushed some of the dirt from her cheek. He allowed his fingertips to linger, then cupped her face in his hands. At that moment he very much wanted to take her in his arms and kiss that delicious-looking mouth. He steeled himself against the temptation and quickly withdrew his hands. He had never before been in the position of wanting to kiss someone so much yet knowing that he didn't dare try.

A shiver tickled across Jessica's nape in response to his touch. It was as unsettling as Dylan himself. She backed away from him. He was as wrong for her as a man could be, yet his mere presence excited her in a way she had never before experienced. She tried to shake off the mesmerizing sensations that enveloped her. It was a bad situation, and it needed to be terminated as quickly as possible.

She took another step away from him as she rubbed her hand across her nape to still the tremor. ''Well…'' She shoved down the sudden nervousness that jittered through her body. She could still feel the heat generated by his touch. ''There's a mess that needs to be cleaned.'' She returned to the living room, leaving Dylan standing on the porch.

He watched her retreating form. His gaze traced the line of her hip and the curve of her bottom beneath the well-worn denim. The tightness spread across his chest, and the heat settled low inside him. Even his fingertips tingled from the brief contact with her cheek. Jessica McGuire was as tantalizingly desirable as any woman he had ever met, yet so unlike any woman he had ever been with. He shook his head as he followed her inside. He needed to add structure and purpose to his life, not complicate it by making a pass at this woman…who also happened to be his best friend's sister.

Jessica purposely kept her distance from Dylan while they cleaned up the mess as best they could. By the time they finished, it was nearly noon. The entire morning had been devoted to one disaster after another. A new layer of anxiety built up on the already established base. Her neat and tidy existence had been turned into a shambles by Dylan Russell, and she did not like it. And worse yet, she didn't know what to do about it. She could still feel his fingertips on her cheek and the heat of his touch.

Dylan was aware of her every movement and gesture, her body language telling him she was out of patience with the series of minidisasters. He made the decision to retreat and give her a little bit of time to calm down. He adopted the facade of the world-weary traveler who had seen it all and done it all. He glanced around the room, satisfied that it was as orderly as possible under the circumstances.

"Things here seem to be under control. I think this would be a good time for me to grab a quick shower." He disappeared into the bathroom.

Many years ago an awkward fifteen-year-old Jessica had followed him around for an entire weekend like a lovesick puppy, and he had not been able to get rid of her. He remembered how funny Justin thought it had been. Then a year later he saw how much the sixteen-year-old Jessica had blossomed. A four-year age difference wasn't much, but the difference between a sixteen-year-old high school girl and a twenty-year-old college man was considerable. He had not had any interest in asking for trouble by making a pass at an underage girl and especially not his best friend's sister.

His mind drifted back to early that morning as he lay in bed watching her pick up her clothes—the way her T-shirt clung to her curves, her long bare legs, the sexy abandon of her mussed hair. The fifteen-year-old Jessica had been a nuisance. Funny how drastically things had changed. He allowed a brief thought about how he might be able to get her to follow him around like that again.

He stared at his reflection in the mirror, ran his hand across his whisker stubble, then heaved a sigh of resignation. Absolutely nothing had gone in his favor since he had gotten out of bed that morning. Actually, nothing had gone in his favor for the past three months. He clicked on his electric razor, hoping the battery had enough charge left for him to shave.

Jessica heard the shower go on. Finally, a chance for some peace and quiet without the distraction of Dylan Russell to set her heart pounding and her pulse racing. She poured herself another cup of coffee, turned on the battery-operated radio, then curled up in the corner of the couch. She reflected on the morning's activities. All she had wanted was a couple of days of quiet and solitude. That was not asking too much, was it? Instead everything seemed to be conspiring against her. She had found herself enmeshed in one calamity after another. First it was the rain as she drove to the cabin, then finding the power out when she had arrived and finally total bedlam masquerading in the person of Dylan Russell.

It was an impossible situation. He would have to leave as soon as he finished in the bathroom. It was bad enough to wake up in the same bed with him by accident, but to allow him to continue to stay in her cabin was out of the question. Determination took a strong hold. Her mind was made up. She would be tactful, but firm. Maybe Justin had promised him the use of the cabin, but even Dylan should be able to recognize what an impossible situation they had.

Then that same determined mind drifted back to the moment when she woke that morning to find his arm curled around her waist and his body snuggled against hers. She could still feel the sensual warmth that radiated from his bare skin in those moments of half sleep and half wakefulness. She vividly recalled each and every plane, angle and line of his well-defined torso when he had propped himself up on his elbow and flashed that deliciously wicked grin. Rogue, scoundrel, playboy, charmer—whatever word you wanted to use, it personified Dylan Russell to a T. No way was he the type of man she could ever be seriously interested in, the kind who would be happy to settle down with a home and family—no way at all.

She shook off the thoughts and the mental image, then took another swallow of her coffee as if trying to drown out her errant musings. She reaffirmed her resolve. Her mind was made up. He definitely had to go, and the sooner the better. Her decision was final. There was no way she would change her mind—no way at all.

A second later, in an act of total defiance against

her rising anxiety. "Well, I just think you'd be more comfortable at the lodge. It's only a few miles from here, down on the main road."

"No. I wouldn't be more comfortable at the lodge."

"What?" She snapped her head in his direction as the shock spread through her body. His words caught her totally off guard. His unwavering gaze provided no hint of what he was thinking, yet it set her anxieties on edge. She stared at the lamp again, unable to hold the directness of his eye contact. There was nothing tentative or unsure about his attitude or the physical stance of his body language.

She forced her words, even though she knew they sounded less firm than when she started. "The lodge is very nice. I'm also sure it will be much more to your liking than being here without any activities or other people to socialize with."

He folded his arms across his chest and leaned against the wall. His voice was calm and very matter-of-fact, his words firm without being argumentative. "This cabin is only half yours. The other half belongs to Justin. You informed him you would be in New York for three weeks. So, taking you at your word, he promised use of the cabin to me. Since you're the one who showed up without checking first, I believe I have the right to stay."

She grabbed the fireplace poker and jabbed at the remnants of the morning's disastrous fire in an effort to play for time as she carefully chose her words. She didn't want to get into an argument, but she wanted to make her position clear. She turned to face him.

"Whether I'm supposed to be in New York or not isn't the point. The fact is that I'm not in New York...I'm here." She caught the edge surrounding her voice and took a steadying breath in hopes of smoothing it out. "I'm truly sorry this unfortunate situation had to occur, but I really do feel that the lodge will be far more to your liking. This cabin certainly can't be the kind of place where you would usually stay. This type of isolation must be quite different from your normal routine."

She wrinkled her brow in concentration for a moment. "In fact, I can't imagine why you would want to stay here at all."

A spark of anger flared with his words. "My *normal routine* has its times of isolation." He paused and took a deep breath before muttering, "But I'm sure you wouldn't understand that."

She saw something in his eyes and heard it for a brief moment in his voice. A hint of vulnerability? As quickly as it materialized it quickly disappeared, to be replaced by a facade of calm control. It was just a glimpse, but enough to tell her that there was more going on inside his head than he was saying or willing to show. What was he hiding? Then another thought occurred to her. Rather than hiding something, could he be hiding from someone?

She had no idea what he had specifically been doing over the years, only what her brother had told her. Perhaps his "business deals" were really scams to fleece unsuspecting people out of their money. A sick churning in the pit of her stomach told her just how much she hoped that wasn't true. She studied him for a moment. He looked so calm and collected, as if nothing could ruffle him. She wished she felt as in control as he looked.

It didn't matter to Dylan how much she pushed him, there was no way he had any intention of staying at a lodge surrounded by the distraction of vacationing people who were there to enjoy themselves. Nor did he want to end up confined inside the four walls of a hotel room in order to have quiet and solitude. And the small apartment he maintained in Los Angeles wasn't as large as the cabin. It was hardly anything more than a place to change clothes and grab a night's sleep between flights to some exotic vacation locale or an international business meeting. The idea of pacing the floor of his apartment surrounded by other buildings in traffic-congested Los Angeles didn't work for him at all. Justin's mountain cabin in the middle of the forest was the ideal solution to his needs. And even with Jessica there, it was still much better than any of the other options.

Or perhaps it was *because* of Jessica being there.

A little shiver of panic darted through his body in response to the unwelcome thought. It was more than wanting the use of the cabin, he *needed* it. He hadn't even informed Justin of exactly how much he needed to be away from everything, to think out his life and make decisions. He knew his best bet was to offer her a compromise, to try to convince her to do it his way, even though her expression projected a stubborn determination that left him uneasy.

He relaxed his stance, unfolded his arms and softened his manner as he crossed the room toward her. He turned on the charm that had served him so well over the years. "There's no reason for this to be causing such a big problem. This cabin is large enough to easily accommodate both of us without our being crowded together." He warmed to the idea, his voice taking on a seductive quality. "You have your bedroom, and I've already moved my things to the other

one. I think we can coexist without any problems.''
He flashed his best *trust me* smile. ''Don't you
agree?''

She stared at him with her mouth hanging open. She
finally managed to say something, but her tone was
more stunned than aggressive. ''You're actually sug-
gesting that we share the cabin? Stay here together?''

''It worked out okay last night when we shared a
bed. I would think sleeping in separate rooms would
make it even easier.'' The memory of their bodies nestled together under the blankets came rushing back to
him full force. He managed to hide his decidedly lusty
thoughts and feelings. The last thing he wanted to do
was give her cause for alarm.

''We didn't share a bed!'' The crimson flush of embarrassment spread across her cheeks, her features ex-
pressing shock and concern.

He couldn't stop his amused reaction. ''We
didn't?'' He shoved back the chuckle that tried to escape. ''Then what would you call it when we both
woke up in the same bed? And remember, I was the
one in there first. You crawled in bed with me, not the
other way around.''

She mustered all the reserved control she could pull
together, looked him squarely in the eyes and said,
''I'd call it a miscalculation.''

This time he couldn't stop the laugh—an open, easy
laugh tinged with a sexy undertone more in line with
fun than a threat. ''You can call it whatever you'd like,
but facts are facts. I'm willing to trust you to behave
properly during the next few days. So, what do you
say? Do we have a deal?''

''*You're* willing to trust *me?*'' Her words came out
in an angry rush. ''Don't you have that a little bit

backward? After all, I'm not the one with the reputation as an international playboy and globe-trotting wheeler-dealer out for a quick buck wherever it can be found.''

It was all he could do to keep from outwardly flinching as the barbed sting penetrated his composure. Her words scored a direct hit. He didn't want to hear them. He knew there was more truth to it than not, but that didn't make it any easier to take. He swallowed down the discomfort her words had caused.

''Well, *Ms.* McGuire,'' he tried to maintain a brisk attitude even though the sting of her words continued to ring in his ears, ''I'm not the only one here with a reputation. Yours is different from mine, but it's a reputation nonetheless…organized, no nonsense, compulsively all business—'' he eyed her curiously ''—and no spontaneity or fun?'' He knew he shouldn't be antagonizing her. He tried to soften the edges on what he'd said. ''We're both adults, and I'm sure we can behave accordingly. I'm willing to take a chance.''

He forced the practiced smile that had never failed to elicit confidence from those on the receiving end, something that had always worked in his favor when putting together one of his business deals. ''How about you?''

''That's absurd.'' Jessica did not know what to make of this strange turn of events. She needed a moment to think. She didn't know which disturbed her more, the circumstances or his comments about her reputation. Did she really come off that way? An uptight workaholic who didn't know how to enjoy herself? She pushed the disagreeable notion away. There wasn't any truth to it. He was just trying to put her on the defensive with his comments. She filled the awkward lull by taking a couple of oil lamps from a cupboard in preparation for nightfall should the electricity not be restored.

She finally turned her attention to Dylan again. "I just don't see how this can—"

The announcement on the radio grabbed their total attention. Because of the high water and debris washing downstream, the bridge over the creek—the only way back to the main road by car—had been closed until further notice. They stared at each other for a moment as the reality sank in, neither of them knowing what to say.

Her anxiety sprang to the forefront and her throat went dry. An unwanted quaver crept into her voice. "It...uh...appears that the decision has been taken out of our hands."

He saw the wariness in her eyes and felt it in the unsettled nervousness tugging at his senses. A hard band tightened across his chest. He didn't know whether to be pleased or apprehensive by the unexpected turn of events. The words tried to choke off in his throat as the full implication hit him. "So it seems."

Jessica's gaze locked with Dylan's, sending a shiver up her spine. She rubbed her hand across her nape in an effort to still the unwanted sensation, but couldn't break away from the magnetic pull of his presence. She experienced a shortness of breath and her heartbeat increased noticeably, much to her regret. She couldn't stop the hint of panic that grew with each passing minute. The news about the bridge was the last thing she wanted to hear.

She tried to gather her composure in spite of the uncertainty that had invaded the very core of her existence. Being temporarily marooned was not of major consequence, but being confined to a cabin with someone who was undeniably the sexiest man she had ever met—a man who was wrong for her in every way—was quite another. His allure was far too tempting. The prospects of what could happen and where things could go truly frightened her.

Her thoughts returned to that morning in her bedroom—the warmth of his body snuggled against hers, the feel of his hand sliding across her waist. A rush of excitement surged through her, suppressing her attempts to deny her desires.

If she had any hopes of making it through this awkward situation, she needed to keep her wits about her and not allow his presence to sway her determination. Regardless of how attractive she found him, she had to resist those desires. In order to ignore the obvious charms of Dylan Russell she needed to pull herself together…and quickly.

"Well, as long as we're stuck here *temporarily*—" she shot him a warning look that said she was in no mood for any arguments "—I think we need to establish some rules." If only she felt as confident as she tried to appear. Yes, they needed some rules, but more to bring logic to her confusion about Dylan and how it was possible for her to be consumed by thoughts of someone she knew was so wrong for her, than anything else.

She watched him for a moment. He did not show any outer reaction to her statement. Her confidence started to rebuild. Maybe she was making more out of this than it deserved. Could it be the same as all those years ago when he asked her to lunch? Was he just trying in his own way to be nice to his friend's sister and make the best of the unusual circumstances? As he'd said, they were both adults. True, they were stuck with an unusual situation, but that didn't mean...

Another shiver of trepidation confirmed what she already knew. It didn't matter how much she tried to lie to herself and how much she wanted to believe that lie, she knew the crush of that teenage girl from many years ago had been resurrected from its dormant state. She had never fully gotten Dylan Russell out of her system. He was the wrong man for her in every sense of the word. In fact, he was the wrong man for any woman who wanted a stable, lasting relationship. But knowing it didn't change the way the tingle of excitement raced through her body every time he looked at her.

She tried to impose a sensible reality to what was happening. She nervously cleared her throat. "I work in public relations—"

"Really?" He cocked his head and raised a questioning eyebrow.

She frowned at him, uncertain about what he meant. "Why does that seem so difficult for you to believe?"

Dylan shrugged in an offhand manner as if her question had no particular relevance to anything, while quickly taking stock of the situation. To say what had popped into his mind, that she had been behaving far too antagonistically for someone whose job included the need to be amiable and occasionally calm stormy waters, would serve no purpose. "I'm just a little surprised, that's all. Justin had never mentioned what you did for a living. Go ahead with what you were saying...something about needing rules."

He was not happy with the hint of anxiety that tried to force its way to the surface. Up until now there had been options available, choices open to each of them about staying at the cabin or leaving. However, in the blink of an eye the situation had changed drastically. The choices had been taken away. The option of leaving no longer existed for either of them.

Under normal circumstances being stranded in an isolated cabin with a very desirable woman would have been a pleasant interlude, but he didn't know what to call this. It was a predicament that could not be taken lightly. It was also a situation filled with possibilities while at the same time fraught with emotional peril. He didn't need any additional upheaval in his life, especially now...regardless of how attractive and incredibly desirable he found her.

He reached out and lightly touched her cheek, trailed his fingers through her hair, then cupped her chin in his hand. He plumbed the depths of her blue eyes. The tightness pulled across his chest again, accompanied by a shortness of breath and a disturbingly heated rush low in his body. Everything about her excited him far more than he wanted it to...and it scared him. He withdrew his hand, forcing himself to break contact with the silky smoothness of her skin.

"You...uh, you were saying? Something about rules?" A touch of huskiness clung to his words.

"Saying?" Her heart pounded in her chest. Surely he must be able to hear it. "Yes...uh...rules." The sensual warmth of his touch lingered on her senses. She reinforced her determination. She had to get her mind back on business. She took a steadying breath.

"I work in public relations which means I spend a lot of time smiling and being gracious to people that I'd sometimes rather ignore. I'm not interested in spending what I thought was going to be my private getaway time at my own cabin by being gracious and playing hostess to a...a *guest.*"

"That's it? Those are the rules?" An amused grin tugged at the corners of his mouth, covering the wave of relief that rippled through him. He had been braced for something monumental, not something so obvious. "I certainly don't have any problem with that. In fact, I insist that you not consider me a guest. I can entertain myself and we can split the chores." He extended a tentative smile. "Agreed?" He held out his hand.

She hesitated, then accepted his outstretched hand. It started as a businesslike handshake, then a second later the sensual warmth totally enveloped her. Logic screamed at her to break the physical contact and back away from him. But just as the moth was drawn to the flame, Dylan Russell's smooth charm and sexy masculinity drew in her emotions and she felt helpless to prevent it.

Then reality hit her when she realized she was being physically pulled toward him as well.

The look in his eyes told her exactly what was on his mind, yet it was not a look of lust or quick sexual conquest. It was a sensual intensity that she had not been prepared for, one that left her gasping for air. A moment later the space between them disappeared and she felt her body come into contact with his. She desperately wanted to break free of his hold before it was too late, but all she could do was stand there, her body pressed against his, and look up into the mesmerizing magic of his eyes.

What if he tried to kiss her? She honestly didn't know if she had the ability to stop him. She wasn't all that sure she had the desire to stop him, either. She made a feeble attempt at putting an end to the emotionally charged moment crackling between them. Her words came out as a mere whisper.

"Food...we haven't eaten anything all day...we, uh—"

"You're right." Two words was all he could manage without giving away too much of what was going on inside him. He hadn't meant to do it, to pull her body against his. Once he had clasped her hand it all seemed to happen of its own volition. He felt her breathing and also felt her tremble. She heated up his desires in a way no other woman ever had. But was this really the time or the place? He didn't have a clue about what to do. He had never before been so uncertain about how to proceed with a woman.

She felt warm, soft and inviting. She was also a four-alarm explosion warning him of sure danger if he didn't let go of her that instant. He released her hand from his grasp and stepped back. He managed to get out some words, not really fully conscious of exactly what he was saying.

"I brought some food with me, but only enough for a couple of days. I noticed you had a supply of canned and packaged foods that don't require refrigeration..." His voice trailed off as he continued to gaze into her eyes. The uncomfortable tightness spread across his chest, once again affecting his breathing. He reached out and brushed his fingertips lightly across her cheek. He had never wanted to kiss anyone as much as he wanted to kiss her at that moment.

The sensual electricity and sexual tension crackled through the air, the atmosphere inside the cabin more charged than the storm outside. He had never met anyone like her. The harder he tried to be charming, the more she resisted his efforts. There was an honesty about her that touched the depths of his soul. She made no effort to be anything other than who and what she was. He found it such a refreshing change of pace from the type of women he had been with in the past.

A touch of melancholy attached itself to his thoughts. Perhaps his judgment of women wasn't all that good. He'd been totally taken in by his ex-fiancée, believed her to be someone she wasn't and ended up paying a huge emotional price for his lack of judgment. He had vowed never again to let his guard down where women were concerned. So what was he doing now? He took another step back, putting some much-needed space between himself and Jessica.

"Lunch…" It was as much a question as a statement, but either way he didn't finish it.

Jessica fought to catch her breath and calm her racing pulse. She had never been so confused about a man in her life. Even with the series of minor catastrophes that had taken up the morning, she could certainly see where his presence would be a temptation to most women. *Most women,* of course, couldn't possibly include her. Her crush had been that of an impressionable teenager on an older college man. It had nothing to do with here and now.

She was far too sensible and mature to become involved with the likes of Dylan Russell no matter how charming, sexy and handsome he was. At least that's what she kept telling herself. But every time that sexy smile lit up his handsome face and the devilish twinkle came into his eyes, she felt herself being drawn closer and closer to what she knew would be the worst thing she could possibly do…and probably the most exciting time of her life.

Dylan directed his outward efforts to the concerns

of the moment. "I brought a few fresh food items, primarily some breakfast things for this morning, plus some canned goods. I put the eggs and butter in the refrigerator when I arrived yesterday evening. Of course, that was before the power went out. The refrigerator door hasn't been opened since then, so I imagine there's still enough cold in there that they're okay."

She furrowed her brow into a slight frown. "Did you bring any fresh meat, chicken or fish? Or any frozen items? The stuff you mentioned should be okay, but the other is a different problem."

"I had planned to go to the market this morning after checking to see what was here." He glanced out the window at the steady downpour. "Obviously a plan that didn't work out."

"I'll make some more coffee."

"And I'll fix some eggs." He started toward the refrigerator then glanced back at her. "Is scrambled okay with you?"

Jessica settled into the corner of the living room couch with her book, leaving Dylan to his own devices.

He brought in more firewood from the porch and set about making another stab at building a fire in the fireplace. Keeping physically busy would help the time pass, but it did nothing to ease his thoughts or help with his inner turmoil. This wasn't what he had bargained for when he arrived at the cabin. He had not been prepared for anyone else to be there, let alone the very disconcerting presence of Jessica McGuire. He had decisions to make with too much riding on the outcome—a new direction for the future and possibly his entire life. He had already put some thoughts together, but it was a long way from being a solid plan.

He watched the fire until he was satisfied that the flue was cleared out enough so the smoke wouldn't back up into the room again. Then the restlessness settled over him. He wandered around the cabin, making a closer inspection of the items in the living room and dining room. He went back to the kitchen and poured a mug of fresh coffee, then carried it toward the stairs. He had told Jessica that the cabin was large enough for two people. Maybe if he put some of that distance between himself and this fascinating woman he'd be able to concentrate.

Nervous energy ran rampant through his body. He paused at the bottom step and stared at her for a moment, his gaze lingering on the way she curled into the corner of the couch. He shoved down the rush of excitement that told him exactly how he would like to work off that excess energy. He sucked in a calming breath, turned and continued up the stairs.

He stood just inside the sliding door to the deck, watching as the rain pelted against the glass. He tried to concentrate his thoughts toward his current problems—what specific goals he wanted to accomplish, what changes he needed to make in order to accomplish those goals, how to put those changes into effect. He paced up and down in front of the glass door, turning several things over in his mind before finally retreating to Justin's bedroom. He stretched out on the bed, stared up at the ceiling and listened to the rain.

It was no use. He couldn't relax…he couldn't think. He was soon up and pacing the floor again—past Jessica's bedroom to the door leading to the deck, back to Justin's bedroom, then toward the deck again. And all the while his thoughts centered more on Jessica than on formulating his plans for the future. He shook his head. She had him so wrapped up in confusion that he couldn't focus on anything else.

After half an hour of pacing and mentally kicking himself, he went back downstairs. He watched her out of the corner of his eye as he tended to the fire. She was exactly where she had been when he went upstairs, still curled up in the corner of the couch reading her book. He envied the way she was able to block out everything and concentrate on reading. He stoked the burning logs and placed another one on the fire.

He wandered across the room, paused by the front door to look out the window, then continued on to the kitchen. He poured himself a cup of coffee, then stood at the kitchen door watching Jessica again. He had brought more with him than just a minimal amount of food supplies. He had also brought some bottles of wine. Perhaps a glass of wine as a peace offering to ease some of the awkward tension that had persisted through the morning?

A glass of wine, the sound of the rain on the roof, a beautiful woman snuggled next to him in front of a cozy fire…it was a real life scene he had played hundreds of times, but never with someone like Jessica McGuire. He looked away as he tried to fight off the growing desires coursing through his body. He wandered over to the fireplace again, then finally settled down on the bottom step of the stairs leading up to the loft. He sipped his coffee, but five minutes later he was back on his feet.

He reminded Jessica of a caged animal—restless, pacing the floor, upstairs then downstairs, in the kitchen then back in the living room, unable to sit still

for more than a few minutes at a time. She had been
trying to concentrate on her book, but had read the
same page three times and still didn't know what it
said. She finally gave up and set the book aside. Trying to concentrate on anything with Dylan in the room
was next to impossible. It was more than his tantalizing allure and the way he sent flutters of excitement
coursing through her veins that she found distracting.

A wave of disgust swept through her. This was her
cabin. She refused to be relegated to the confines of
her bedroom in order to read a book. He said he would
entertain himself and she wouldn't even know he was
there. Well, so far he had been a dismal failure at both.
He didn't seem to be making any attempt to entertain
himself, and there was no way she could ignore his
presence…regardless of how much she tried.

She watched him for a couple of minutes before it
dawned on her that he seemed more preoccupied than
merely restless. Her mind turned to Dylan Russell the
man rather than Dylan Russell the distraction. Why
would someone like him want to be in such solitary
circumstances? A man who had turned partying into
an art form was not the type who would want to be
alone. Quite the contrary. That type usually needed to
be surrounded by other people so that they wouldn't
be alone. Yet there he was. He had refused to leave,
refused to consider her option of checking into the
lodge…when it had still been an option.

It was a strange situation, one she didn't understand,
but the more she watched him the more she wanted to
know. It had gone beyond her fascination with a sexy,
desirable man. He had become an enigma. There was
something very real going on inside him and she
wanted to be able to understand it.

He opened the cabin door and wandered out to the porch. She watched him through the window. He appeared temporarily content to stand there, staring at the rain and sipping his coffee. She rose from the couch and joined him, eliciting nothing more than a quick glance acknowledging her presence.

"You seem very restless and preoccupied with something. I suspected the isolation here would not be to your liking. I don't understand why you thought this would be the type of place you would be comfortable with. Even if the power was on, there isn't even a television or VCR. Justin and I agreed that we wanted to use the cabin as a true getaway."

"That's exactly why I wanted to use it, too…it's a true getaway."

She waited, hoping he would offer more information, but he continued to stare out at the rain. "But you seem so restless—"

He jerked around and glared at her. "I wanted to do some hiking, all right?" He hadn't meant to snap out the words like that, cutting her off in midsentence, but his restlessness and inability to concentrate had made him irritable. He glanced at the serious expression on her face and managed a weak smile as he tried to make light of the situation. "Being in the woods, communing with nature…that kind of thing."

"You certainly could have done all the hiking you wanted from the lodge."

He ignored her comment, choosing instead to look up at the stormy sky. "Does it seem like it's letting up a little bit? Maybe we'll be able to see some sun before the day is over."

He knew exactly where she was going with the conversation, wanting to know why he wanted to be at the cabin and had refused to leave, and he didn't want to tread that path again. It was something he hadn't clearly figured out for himself yet and certainly a topic he was not prepared to discuss with anyone else. It was all too personal and came from a place of vulnerability that he didn't want anyone to see. Then he thought of Rose and Stanley Clarkson again. The guilt over what had happened welled inside him, quickly accompanied by his fear over the direction his life was headed if he didn't make some drastic changes. Yes, he had lots of things to work out, and running through it all, clouding his thinking, was something he hadn't planned on…the very real distraction of an intriguing woman who literally took his breath away and made his blood race.

Jessica glanced up at the stormy sky. "I don't think so. We'll be lucky if the rain lets up before morning. Sunshine is an entirely different topic."

She watched him a moment longer as he stared ahead blankly, not acknowledging her comments. She carefully measured her words, wanting to know yet not wanting to antagonize him with her prying. "I still don't understand why you insisted on staying here rather than at the lodge."

He turned his gaze on her, sending a little shiver of anxiety through her body. She wasn't sure what to make of his expression. It was as if he had chosen to no longer accommodate anything other than his own thoughts and concerns. A new level of uncertainty rose inside her, but she refused to allow it to deter her from her goal of finding out why Dylan Russell had shown up out of the clear blue to invade her personal sanctuary.

"There isn't anything here that wouldn't be more

comfortable and convenient for you if you were at the lodge.'' She looked at him questioningly, waiting for a reply.

Something flashed through his eyes but it disappeared before she could read it. Could it have been anger? She shifted her weight uncomfortably under the scrutiny of his unrelenting stare. Had she pushed him too far? A hint of trepidation shivered through her body.

"I don't mean to be rude, but I don't believe my reasons are really any of your business." Dylan turned his gaze away from her, once again seemingly staring out at nothing in particular. "Besides, since neither of us can leave it's a moot point."

Jessica bristled at his attitude. "Quite the contrary...I believe your having climbed into my bed makes it very much my business."

Four

The second the words were out of her mouth Jessica wished she hadn't said them. She vividly recalled the moment Dylan's arm slipped around her waist and the way his body nestled against hers. The sensual heat produced by the memory quickly spread through her body until it touched every part of her existence.

She hated not having any better control over her thoughts and feelings than what had been happening to her since the moment she opened her eyes that morning. She gathered her resolve. Absurd, that's what it was. She was not about to allow her hormones to dictate to her, regardless of how sexy and desirable she found this man.

"The bed was empty when I climbed into it." He forced a lightness to his voice, attempting to take the edge off the tenuous situation. "So technically you crawled into bed with me." The memory of those early-morning minutes spent snuggled together in a warm bed washed over him. There had been no intentional intimacy between them. It was all very natural and comfortable. It felt very right, not at all the same as with other women over the years.

He regarded her a moment longer. Things were already strained enough without him making it worse. He placed his hand at the small of her back and guided her toward the cabin door. "Come on, let's go inside. It's too cold to be standing out here." He extended an encouraging smile as they stepped back inside. "Besides, there's a perfectly good fire in the fireplace that's going to waste."

Dylan put forth his best effort to be pleasant. He stoked the fire and added another log. "There...that should do it for a while."

Jessica stood in front of the fireplace, hugging her shoulders. "The heat feels good." She rubbed her hands together as her chill began to subside. "I didn't realize how cold it was out there, although I think it's the damp as much as it is the temperature."

"Yes, that damp air has a way of cutting right through you before you realize it, and suddenly you're chilled to the bone and can't seem to get warm again." It was an inane conversation made up of polite yet strained comments. He sauntered across the room to the couch, picked up the book she had been reading and leafed through a couple of pages.

"I've been meaning to read this." He set it down and turned toward her. "Is it any good?"

"Yes, I'm enjoying it. I started it on the flight from New York to Seattle and I'm anxious to finish it." She knew she would enjoy it a lot more if she had been able to concentrate on what she was reading, due only in part to Dylan's restlessness and more to the sensual energy that seemed to emanate from him. "Justin read it and passed it on to me."

His gaze darted around the cabin, not really landing on anything in particular. "How's Justin doing?" He pulled a couple of chairs in front of the fireplace, sat in one and indicated the other one for her. "We didn't get a chance to talk. I sent an e-mail about using the cabin and he sent me the key. In the brief note he enclosed he said he'd been very busy. Is he still flying for the charter company?"

She seated herself in the other chair. It was obvious he was trying to make small talk, something to ease the tension. She knew he was right. Circumstances had marooned them at the cabin. She needed to put forth the same effort. She was very much aware of how close together the chairs were, but it somehow seemed very cozy—the fireplace, the sound of rain on the roof and the most desirable man she had ever encountered seated at her side. So why was she being assaulted by waves of apprehension?

"He's still flying for them. He's been flying his maximum allowed hours plus putting in lots of extra time with other functions. He has an opportunity..." She hesitated, not sure if she should tell Dylan about Justin's plans.

"An opportunity? You mean the partnership? He mentioned it, saying it was something he wanted to check out, but never said anything else about it. Is he going through with it?"

"Well, since he's already said something to you about it, I guess it won't hurt if I fill you in. The information isn't common knowledge yet, so I'd appreciate it if you didn't say anything to anyone."

"No problem. I'm very good at not revealing things that need to be kept private. Most of my business transactions required that type of discretion."

"What's happening right now is that he's buying half the charter company he works for, with a five-year option to buy out the other half at a predetermined price. He looked at it from all angles and finally decided to go through with the deal. As the senior pilot he's been able to pretty much set his own schedule, take the flights he wanted and be off when he wanted. As one of the owners it will mean a lot more responsibility and a long-term commitment."

A subdued laugh escaped Dylan's throat, one of irony more than amusement. "Funny the way things turn around—" he became reflective as he stared at the flames "—sometimes when you least expect it."

"Oh? Like what?" She cocked her head and looked at him, her keen interest in what he had said written all over her features.

He ignored her question, once again sidestepping her attempt to delve into what he considered private matters. He felt much more comfortable discussing something *safe* like Justin's plans. "Will being one of the owners mean that he won't be able to take any more of the flights himself? I know how much he loves to fly."

"That was one of the considerations he had to deal with. He won't be able to take as many flights, but it's something that will allow him to plan for the future and build a career should something happen that would prevent him from being able to fly. He gave it a lot of thought. We discussed it several times, and he finally decided to make the commitment. He plans to buy out the other half of the company as quickly as possible.''

A hint of a smile tugged at the corners of her mouth. ''He hasn't said so, but I know he's a little worried about being able to come up with the money to exercise his option on the other half. He doesn't want to incur an unreasonable amount of debt, but he doesn't want to let this deal slip away, either. It's really a terrific opportunity. I've thought about maybe taking all my savings and investing in the company as a 10 percent owner which will help ease the amount of money he needs.'' The smile soon became a soft laugh. ''It's interesting to think of being business partners with Justin, but it's certainly a possibility....''

He reached out and gently touched her cheek. His voice held a tenderness that surprised even him. ''That's the first time I've seen you smile since we woke up this morning.'' He plumbed the depth of her eyes while trying to ignore the surge of desire pushing at his senses. ''You have a lovely smile. You should do it more often.''

He saw her uncertainty and quickly withdrew his hand. He stared ahead at the flames. He became reflective and somewhat distracted as he voiced his thoughts. ''Interesting that Justin should be thinking and planning for the future beyond being a pilot. I've...uh...sort of been doing a little of that myself lately.'' It was an admission he hadn't intended to make, but the words had just sort of slipped out.

He quickly covered his inadvertent comment by pursuing the interesting bit of information she had given him. ''How does he plan to finance the buyout? Is he okay right now for purchasing half, with exercising the option as the only problem?''

"I'm not really sure. Why do you ask?"

"I can help him with the financing, both now and the additional amount he'll need later."

"You mean…uh …" She was not sure how to word it so it didn't sound like an accusation. "You mean by making this one of your *business deals?*"

He turned in his chair until he directly faced her again. He studied her for a moment. Her expression was more one of wariness than it was antagonism. "You say that as if you were accusing me of doing something illegal…or at the very least unethical." He studied her for a moment before answering her question. "No, I meant I'd lend him the money if he needs it."

Her eyes widened in shock. "But there's a great deal of money involved…you don't even know how much he needs."

"You're right, I don't know how much money we're talking about." He had been too comfortable sitting in front of the fire talking quietly with her and had allowed himself to become vulnerable to her questions. He didn't know what to say, how much to reveal. Should he say the simple truth, that he was a multimillionaire with a great deal of his fortune able to be quickly converted into cash? He decided against it. He didn't want to take a chance on her misinterpreting what he said, of her thinking he was trying to buy Justin's gratitude. Or worse yet…hers.

He reached out and brushed his fingertips across her cheek. Once again the band tightened across his chest. What he had told Jessica about being discreet had been true. He never discussed his business deals with anyone other than those directly involved in the transactions. He never discussed his personal finances with anyone.

"How can you say you'd lend him the money if you don't have any idea how much it would be?" The warmth of his touch sent tremors of excitement through her body as his fingertips lingered against her cheek. What was there about Dylan Russell that cut through her down-to-earth common sense and knocked her for a loop? Whatever it was, it frightened her emotionally while at the same time holding her in the grip of his physical nearness as sure as if he had been actually restraining her.

"I guess I meant I'd do what I could to see that he was able to make the purchase." He slid his fingers along her jaw, then cupped her chin in his hand. His voice dropped to a soft, seductive tone. "I'd hate to see him miss out on something this important if there was anything I could do to help."

Her words came out in a breathless whisper. "That's very nice of you to offer."

"Justin is my friend…my best friend." A lump formed in his throat. A rush of sadness filled him as the remaining words escaped in a quiet hush, so low that they were almost inaudible. "Perhaps my only true friend." He chased the moment of melancholy away before it overwhelmed him.

He leaned forward until he was within inches of her face. He wanted so much to kiss her, to taste the delicious-looking mouth that had been driving him crazy all day. The uncertainty that had earlier invaded his consciousness once again returned to plague him.

"How about you, Jessica?" He succumbed to the urge as he brushed his lips lightly against hers. He didn't dare allow the gesture to linger in the form of a true kiss, even though it was what he wanted to do. "Are you my friend, too?"

He saw the same bewilderment mirrored in her eyes that clouded his own senses. Had he just made a colossal mistake? He had never experienced quite that reaction to a woman. She was the type with which he had no experience—honest, self-reliant, capable and down-to-earth—qualities he found very appealing. It was more than merely wanting to get a beautiful woman into bed. It was so much more. What was happening was as frightening to him as it was intriguing.

And lurking in the middle of his physical attraction to her was a growing awareness of how easy it would be for the physical desires to turn into an emotional involvement…something he knew all too well had to eventually lead to some sort of a commitment. He had been down that road before. He led with his heart and it had taken him all the way to the altar, then kicked him in the teeth and left him a member of the walking wounded. It had been a painful lesson, and one he had carried with him all these years. It was an experience he didn't want to repeat.

Then, as if on cue, that vacant spot in his life he wanted to fill jabbed at his awareness, quickly followed by an invisible shiver of panic. Another roadblock flew in his face in the form of a nagging reminder that she was more than just another woman. Even though she was no longer an underage teenager, she was still Justin's sister. He already had enough guilt to wrestle with over what had happened to Stanley and Rose Clarkson because of him. He didn't need to further compound his self-created upheaval. But all those good intentions didn't shake his thoughts about her or lessen the possibilities that he knew would present themselves as the evening unfolded.

For the first time in his adult life he didn't know what to do or how to proceed where a woman was concerned. Perhaps he had already done too much. He tentatively reached out and framed her face with his hands. Her slightly parted lips seemed to be beckoning him forward in spite of the wariness in her eyes and the caution blanketing her features. He closed his eyes for a moment, took a calming breath, then backed off.

The subdued daylight that had fought its way through the gloominess of the storm was fading into evening. Somehow over the course of a tension-filled day she had invaded his senses totally and completely. Now that night approached and they had settled into a more comfortable mode of easy conversation, the temptation of her nearness had become almost irresistible. But unlike the others over the years, he could not assume anything with her.

He nervously cleared his throat and tried to bring a sense of calm to the anxiety that fueled his confusion. "I'd better bring in some more wood." He rose from the chair, took the poker and jabbed at the last burning log.

"That's...uh...a good idea." She ran her hand across her nape, but it did nothing to still the tremors that materialized the moment he touched her. She skimmed her fingertips across her lips. She could still feel the heat of his touch. When he brushed his mouth against hers it had literally taken her breath away.

"While you're doing that I'll get out the oil lamps." She spotted the lamps she had already taken from the cupboard. "I mean..." Her gaze darted nervously around the room. Apprehension churned in the pit of her stomach. She felt totally lost as if she were trying to find her way through unfamiliar territory. "I'd better find the bottle of lamp oil, some more matches and check on batteries for the flashlight and the radio."

She had never had anyone rattle her composure the way he did. She tried to tell herself it was nothing more than an understandable reaction to a very sexy man, not any different from being aware of the latest heart throb movie star. It was nothing personal and certainly not with a man so blatantly wrong for her in every way possible or for that matter wrong for any woman who wanted a commitment to a true relationship. At least that was what she kept trying to tell herself.

And each time she tried, she knew it was a lie.

She watched him as he carried in an armload of wood and put it on the hearth next to the fireplace. He added a couple of logs to the fire, then stared at it for a few seconds. Everything about him excited her. No man had ever left her nerve endings tingling or her lungs gasping for air the way he did.

"There." He turned to face her, extending a casual smile. "That should last us for a while." He checked his watch. "At least until bedtime..." His smile faded as their gazes locked.

The electricity crackled between them, filling the air with a sensual heat that neither of them could ignore or deny. He took a couple of steps toward her and held out his hand. It was as if he no longer had control of his actions. He grasped her hand in his, then laced their fingers together. No man in his right mind could ignore this beautiful and desirable woman.

"Did you find the lamp oil and batteries?" He knew it was a stupid question, but he felt pressured to say something in an attempt to ease the pounding in his chest.

"Uh…yes, they're on the kitchen counter."

He led her back to the chairs in front of the fireplace. "Make yourself comfortable." He glanced toward the window where the last remnants of daylight showed the rain hitting against the panes of glass. Light and shadow flickered around the walls, the fireplace providing the only illumination in the room. "I brought some bottles of wine with me. A glass of wine should fit right in with a rainy night and a nice fire, don't you think? It will give us a chance to talk…to get to know each other a little better." He smiled encouragingly, not at all sure where he was going with any of this.

She tried to speak, but no words came out. Her throat closed off when she attempted to swallow. A shortness of breath caught in her lungs. She nodded her head in agreement, unable to manage anything else. He had charmed his way into her life, and she didn't know how to stop it…or if she even wanted it stopped.

Dylan disappeared into the kitchen and returned a few minutes later carrying two glasses of wine. He handed one of them to her, then seated himself in the other chair. He held out his glass toward her. "Let's drink to discovering new friends."

He cocked his head and looked at her questioningly. He dropped his voice to a seductive whisper as he delved into the depth of her eyes. The uncertainty and the tenuous nature of the situation quickly swept over him. The tightness pulled across his chest again, a sensation that repeated whenever he got too near to Jessica. "And to the promise of what the future holds?"

She raised her glass to meet his, even though she didn't have control over the tremor that caused her hand to shake just a little. She repeated his words, forcing her voice to climb above a whisper. "To discovering new friends."

He took a sip from his glass, then settled back in his chair. "Tell me about yourself, Jessica. What have you been doing since you were sixteen years old? You're using the name McGuire…does that mean you've never married?"

"I took back my maiden name when I got divorced seven years ago." She took a sip of her wine. A soft warmth drifted over her, but it failed to drive away the unsettled tremors warning her against getting too comfortable around this man. "What about you? Have you ever been married?"

"Marriage is for suckers."

His blunt statement caught her by surprise. "That's a pretty cynical attitude."

"Perhaps." He reflected on his comment for a moment, then quickly turned the conversation back to her. "You're divorced? Do you have any children?"

"No…" She clenched her jaw for a moment before relaxing the facial expression that spoke to him of past hurts and some still-unresolved issues. The bitterness of deep wounds surrounded her words. "My *ex* wasn't interested in having a family."

The brief glimpse of her pain touched a spot deep inside him. He caressed her cheek, touched her hair, then trailed his fingertips down the side of her neck before relinquishing the sensation. His words were more whispered than spoken. "I'm sorry it didn't work out for you."

It was a moment of emotional intimacy, a totally

spontaneous gesture brought on by a sense of shared disappointment and loss. He drew in a steadying breath in a futile attempt to calm the unsettled feelings racing around inside him, but it didn't help. It was an urgency that wanted so much more than to merely feel the texture of her skin. The heat of the brief moment when he brushed his lips against hers came rushing back at him.

He swallowed down the lump in his throat as he struggled for something to say…anything to keep him from doing what he really wanted to do. "You…you said you work in public relations. Do you have your own company?"

"I'm a freelance consultant, so I guess that makes it my own company, even though I'm not an incorporated business. I'm contracted per project rather than being on staff somewhere."

"Do you enjoy it?"

The sensation of his touch still lingered on her cheek, sending shivers of excitement rippling across her skin. Her breath caught in her lungs. She took a sip of her wine. The seductive atmosphere was tantalizing, yet much too disturbing. He was her ex-husband all over again—the same type of handsome features, the charming manner and flagrantly womanizing ways.

Dylan Russell was absolutely wrong for her. His type of man would never be content to give up his globe-trotting ways, to settle down to a life of responsibility and commitment, any more than her ex-husband had been willing to accept the responsibilities of marriage and commitment. So why did his mere touch make her tremble with anticipation about what might be? It was a question she did not want to dwell on.

She took another drink from her wineglass before replying to his question. "Yes. I enjoy my work very much. I like the challenge and seeing the results of my efforts."

He leaned back in his chair and swirled the wine in his glass, staring at the rich red color until it came to rest before he took a drink. His expression turned reflective, his words almost as if he was saying them to himself rather than talking to her. "Being able to stick around to see the successful outcome of your efforts must be very rewarding for you." He took another sip from his glass and stared blankly at the burning logs.

She cocked her head and wrinkled her brow into a frown. He seemed to be a thousand miles away, as if his thoughts were far removed from their conversation. She spoke hesitantly, not sure exactly how to respond to his comment. "That's a sad sort of statement. Don't you ever get to see the outcome of your efforts?"

"Sometimes...well, it's not always possible...." The outcome of his efforts—yes, he definitely had seen the outcome of his *efforts*. He had seen a very nice man and his wife almost financially ruined because of his *efforts*. He drained the last swallow from his wineglass. He didn't know how to answer her without saying more than he was willing to reveal.

He forced a smile and covered his concerns with a practiced charm as he expertly steered the conversation away from himself. "I'd much rather talk about you. How did you get into public relations?"

An announcement on the radio broke into their conversation. Even though the rain had let up considerably where they were, it was still raining hard farther up in the mountains and the bridge would remain closed throughout the night. The widespread power outages would also continue until the storm let up and work crews could get out to make the necessary repairs.

Dylan didn't know if that was what he wanted to hear or not. His time with Jessica had been enough for him to know beyond a shadow of a doubt that if they stayed in the cabin together, regardless of the fact that they had separate bedrooms, he would end up making a very sincere pass at her before the night was over. He also knew that it wouldn't come from a place of fun and games. His greatest fear at the moment was just how real his attraction to her had become and how serious it could end up being.

"Your glass is empty and so is mine." He rose from his chair and took her glass from her hand. "I'll pour us another glass."

"No—" The panic coursed through her body. The gentle patter of rain on the roof, a cozy fire and a man who made her heart pound with excitement—a second glass of wine was probably not the best idea. She looked up into the emerald depths of his eyes and that was all it took. "Well…maybe half a glass."

A warm smile spread across his face. "I'll be right back."

She watched him until he disappeared into the kitchen, then she leaned back in her chair, closed her eyes and expelled the breath she had been holding from the moment he flashed that killer smile. She wasn't a silly teenager. She was a mature woman. So why were her hormones doing flip-flops every time he looked at her?

Five

"**H**ere you go."

The sound of Dylan's voice snapped Jessica to attention. She took the glass from his outstretched hand. "Thank you, although this seems to be more than half a glass."

A mischievous grin tugged at the corners of his mouth. "I guess I forgot."

As much as she wanted to be annoyed by the obvious ploy, his little-boy-who-was-caught-doing-something-naughty expression cut right through her annoyance and touched a warm spot inside her.

"I see. It just sort of slipped your mind?"

He adopted a serious stance as if repelling an accusation. "Are you doubting my integrity?"

"Perhaps." It was certainly a loaded question, one that could produce an unpleasant disagreement or a moment of gentle teasing. There had already been enough strained incidents between them for one day. They were stranded together. No purpose would be served by exacerbating the problem.

She tried, but she couldn't suppress the grin that played across her lips. "Does your integrity fall into doubt very often?"

"Never! I'm known far and wide for my integrity." The brief lighthearted moment suddenly fell serious as his own words hit him hard. A mental image of Stanley and Rose Clarkson popped into his mind. Integrity, indeed! He had done nothing wrong, yet the guilt and remorse continued to twist his insides into knots.

He grabbed the poker and jabbed at the burning logs with a vengeance in an attempt to keep his inner turmoil from showing. The last thing he wanted was for this very together woman to see the vulnerability he worked so hard to keep hidden.

"There." He replaced the poker, pleased with his success at maintaining control of the situation. "That should do it for a while longer—" The words caught in his throat as he turned toward her. The light from the fire bathed her face in a soft golden glow and reflected in the depth of her eyes. He had never seen anything so captivating and beautiful in his entire life. The sight literally took his breath away, leaving him momentarily speechless. He had never wanted anyone as much as he wanted her at that moment.

Panic squeezed his insides. Logic screamed at him to go upstairs and lock himself in Justin's bedroom before he did something foolish—something he knew he would end up regretting. His desires overruled his anxieties, effectively managing to shove his panic aside. He picked up a couple of the large floor pillows stacked against the wall and placed them in front of the hearth. He took the wineglass from her hand and set it on the mantel next to his.

"I believe you were telling me about your public relations work." The huskiness that accompanied his words left him uneasy—a huskiness he feared would belie his outer calm. He took her hand and gave it a gentle tug.

"I think we'd be cozier over here, closer to the fire." Was he asking for more trouble than he already had? Deep down inside he knew the answer, but chose to ignore it.

"I don't know if that's a good idea..." Her words trailed off before she could finish what she was trying to say. He coaxed her to her feet and escorted her the few steps to the floor pillows. The warmth of his touch traveled from her hand, up her arm and spread through her body. It was the type of sensual heat that radiated from the inside, one far more intense than could ever be generated by a fireplace. She feared what the night would bring, but was helpless to resist. She had allowed herself to become trapped in the pull of his magnetic sex appeal.

As soon as she was seated on the pillow he retrieved the wineglasses from the mantel. He handed one of them to her, but seemed somewhat distracted as he settled himself on the other pillow. He furrowed his brow in concentration, took a sip from his glass and stared into the fire as if lost in thought. She studied his profile, the worried expression on his face and his tensed muscles. Something was troubling him. She had seen it earlier, and now she saw it again just as the touches of vulnerability had shown from time to time. Perhaps his life wasn't as charmed as she had assumed.

"Are you okay?"

He glanced in her direction, a hint of confusion covering his features. "Am I okay? Certainly. Why do you ask?"

"You seem...well, sort of preoccupied. Is..." She wasn't sure about how to proceed. "Is there something wrong?" She hesitated, then cautiously asked, "Something you'd like to talk about?" A sadness in his eyes touched a spot deep inside her, a poignancy that connected on a very human level, bypassing the sensual pull and creating a surprising feeling of closeness. She touched his arm and ventured a tentative comment. "I'm a very good listener."

Dylan turned his gaze on her, once again capturing her essence and pulling her very soul into the depths of his eyes. She swallowed hard, but didn't look away. A troubled expression covered his face, a hesitation that said he was turning her words over in his mind. He glanced at the fire for a moment. When he returned his attention to her, all the uncertainty she saw just seconds earlier had been replaced by his easy manner and smooth charm.

"Why would you think something was wrong? What could be better than this? We have a nice fire, a bottle of good wine..." The practiced smile faded. The warmth of his touch spread across her cheek, then his lips were on hers. It was not another quick brushing as before. This was a kiss, a very real kiss that sent a wave of excitement crashing through her body. This was wrong...totally and completely wrong. He was the wrong man. What they were doing was wrong. So why did it feel so very right?

Every doubt she ever had disappeared in a heated rush when he enfolded her into his embrace. He held her body against his, gently caressing her back and shoulders with a touch so sensual that she couldn't have fought it even if she wanted to. She slipped her arms around his neck, returning his kiss with a fervor that spoke volumes about the passion hidden beneath her logical and organized surface.

Dylan twined his fingers in the silky strands of her hair, then sank back into the softness of the floor pillows, taking her with him. His lips nibbled at the corners of her mouth then he recaptured it with a new intensity. Her taste filled him with a need for more. She was every bit as delicious as he knew she would be…and every bit as addictive as he feared. Any thoughts he might have had, any attempt to rationalize his actions, disappeared in a heartbeat…a very excited heartbeat to be sure.

Jessica found herself wrapped in the sensual cocoon that embodied Dylan Russell, a blanket every bit as emotional as it was physical. She had wondered what it would be like to be kissed by him, and she wasn't disappointed. Her heart pounded in her chest. He literally took her breath away, leaving her light-headed. His mouth demanded, yet she didn't feel threatened. He took, but not more than she willingly gave.

She ran her fingers through his thick hair, all the while allowing him to pull her body tighter against his. Never had anything so wrong felt so right. A tremor darted up her spine when he ran his hand under the back of her sweater and across her bare skin. A rush of excitement rippled through her body in the wake of his touch. It spoke to her of the ecstasy that could be, while at the same time leaving her fearful of the consequences.

It had been many years since she had been this attracted to a man. And once again she had gravitated toward a man who showed no interest in the things she felt very strongly about such as commitment, responsibility and honesty in a relationship. Everything she had heard about him said he was far too much like her ex-husband in that regard. She had been there before and didn't want to repeat the mistake, regardless of how much Dylan excited her. Somehow she had to find the inner strength to put a stop to what was happening…somehow, before it was too late. Then, as if a second surge of energy had taken hold, his kiss infused her with a passion unlike anything she had ever before experienced. Any further doubts evaporated.

Her ardent response caught him by surprise. He had given in to a very strong desire, half spontaneous impulse and half conscious method, but had not expected such earthy enthusiasm in return. He *knew* beyond a shadow of a doubt that he shouldn't be doing this and certainly not with this woman, but all the conscious thought in the world didn't change things. She excited him in a way no other woman ever had, an excitement not confined to only physical desires…an excitement so intense that it scared him.

He forced the thoughts from his mind. He didn't want to think and he certainly didn't want to rationalize what he was doing. He wanted only to indulge each and every sensation. He caressed her bare skin beneath her sweater as he slid his hand across her back, then pulled her tighter in his arms. Her breasts pressed against his chest with each breath she took, stimulating his ardor more than he had been prepared to comfortably control. He ran his hand along the curve of her hip, then across her bottom as he snuggled her hips against his.

He kissed his way from her lips to the side of her neck. The soft moan escaped his throat as soon as he relinquished domination of her mouth, quickly followed by a shiver of panic. As sure as he knew his own name, he also knew he had started down a path that could only lead him where he had no business going. Knowing, however, didn't change anything. He continued down that very path, more enthralled with her than he had ever been with any woman.

Jessica's senses whirled in an uncontrolled haze. Little tingles of pure pleasure followed in the wake of his kisses, sending shivers of delight down her back until they reached the warmth of his hand stroking her bare skin. Every excited breath she drew told her making love with Dylan Russell would be an experience beyond anything she had ever known.

Then a hard jolt of fear yanked her back to her senses. She pushed away from him in a near panic to escape the embrace that had propelled her to new heights, if only for a moment. Her heart pounded, but not just from the very persuasive seduction that had almost been her downfall. Fear also pounded in her chest...fear of what he made her feel and how much she would willingly give to him without question.

Her words came out in a breathless rush. "This is wrong. It has to stop." She tried to force a confidence and determination into her voice. She refused to make eye contact with him, knowing she didn't dare allow even that bit of a connection.

"Why?" The huskiness of his voice said more than his words.

She scrambled to her feet. "This is happening much too fast." She nervously smoothed her hair back with her fingers. "Perhaps you're comfortable with life in the fast lane...with easy conquests and recreational sex...but that's not my style.''

He snapped out his response, anger surrounding his words as much as confusion. ''What's that supposed to mean?''

She took a couple of steps away from him, desperate to escape the pull of his sexual energy...the very same irresistible magnetism that had totally captured her in its grasp. She tried her best to project an in-control businesslike manner. ''I'd appreciate it if you'd move your belongings to Justin's bedroom. It's been a long, exasperating day and I'm tired.''

He made no attempt to hide his feelings about her accusations as he snapped out his response. ''I moved my things this morning.''

Surprise shot her gaze toward him, locking with his for a heated second before she forced herself to turn away. He looked so sexy, so desirable...and also angry. She couldn't allow herself to be drawn in again. ''This morning? Before the bridge was even closed?''

He ignored her question as he slowly sat upright while trying to pull his composure together. The anger continued to churn inside him...*easy conquests and recreational sex.* Did she honestly believe that was all he wanted from her? All that mattered in his life?

Her voice had become hesitant. ''I...uh, think it's time to call it a night.''

Her words cut into his thoughts. He saw the uncertainty that blanketed her features, and it softened his anger at bit. Perhaps she had been right in her accusations. It wasn't the way things were now, but he couldn't say that about the past.

''I'll see you in the morning.'' She turned and

walked up the stairs without waiting for him to answer.

He watched her until she was out of sight. He had not been sure how to respond to her accusations or her attitude. One moment she was wrapped in his arms, all the heat and passion any man could want, and the next she was hurling unfair accusations at him. He continued to stare at the top of the staircase, but Jessica did not reappear. He finally rose to his feet, lit the wick of an oil lamp and put out the remains of the fire in the fireplace.

He carried the lamp upstairs, pausing for a moment at her closed door. The passion of the kisses they had shared continued to linger on his senses. He wanted more, but those desires were tempered with caution. Why had she so abruptly broken off their heated yet all too brief liaison, and with such hurtful words?

He knocked softly. "Jessica?"

He waited, but no response came from the other side of the door. He continued on to the other bedroom and set the lamp on the nightstand. A restlessness consumed him, something more than just not being sleepy. He stared out the window into the darkness. It had nearly stopped raining. Maybe morning would put a brighter light on things. He looked around hoping to find something to read. He opened the door in the nightstand, removed a couple of magazines, then replaced them. Then he opened the nightstand drawer.

He could not stop the amused chuckle when he saw the condom packets. Maybe Jessica considered the cabin to be a quiet getaway, but it was obvious that Justin used it as a seductive location for his love life. The chuckle faded as he picked up one of the packets. He glanced toward the bedroom door. She was so near.

A sigh of resignation reverberated through his chest. He put the packet back and slowly closed the drawer.

He undressed and climbed into bed, but sleep eluded him. He couldn't shut off the thoughts about Jessica, about the possibilities presented from their being stranded together. There was one thing that had become very clear to him—there could never be a no-strings-attached affair with her. She was the type of woman who would demand…and he reluctantly allowed that she would also deserve…some sort of commitment. How could he possibly think in terms of a commitment when he had no idea what the future held for him? There was no way he could involve anybody else in his life until he put his own demons of guilt to rest and resolved his emotional fears.

He tried to get his mind off Jessica by concentrating on his plans for the future. He had been turning an idea over in his mind, one that allowed him to give something to the community rather than selfishly indulging only his own interests. The more he honed the rough spots in the plan, the more he liked it.

Had Jessica's presence allowed him to finally bring the plan into clear focus? The notion that she somehow had something to do with his being able to bring the pieces together sent a warm sensation through his body. His tensed muscles loosened up, and the myriad of thoughts circulating through his head took on a much-needed calm. He drifted into a comfortable sleep with reflections of Jessica filtering through the subconscious workings of his mind.

Jessica stood on the porch, watching as the clouds gave way to the early-morning sun. It had all the signs of being a beautiful day with the storm having moved on. She had spent a very restless night trying to justify what had happened. No matter how exciting she found him, she knew if she had allowed things to progress she would inevitably have been filled with regret. She had no intention of being another notch on this playboy's bedpost.

She stared up at the morning sky. The cruel light of dawn had arrived and despite her chosen path she still had regrets, but she wasn't sure exactly why. Were they for what had happened or because she had stopped what could have happened?

"Good morning."

Jessica whirled around at the sound of Dylan's voice. Her pulse shot into high gear the moment she saw him. He appeared well rested, which was more than she could say for herself, and far too tempting. Memories of the heated kisses they had shared ignited her senses, resurrecting the very real excitement from the previous night. She touched her trembling fingertips to her lips, then took a calming breath before she tried to speak.

"Good morning. I...I didn't hear you open the door."

"Here." He handed her a mug of steaming coffee. "I went to the kitchen and saw that the coffee was almost ready, so I waited for it."

"Thanks." She took a sip from the cup. "This hits the spot." Inane small talk...she knew she sounded like an idiot. If only she could have thought of something intelligent to say, something that would have conveyed her control of the situation...something that would have let him know that his kisses had no effect on her. If only she could convince herself of that, too.

He glanced up at the clear sky. "Looks like the

storm has moved on." He returned his attention to Jessica. "I'm putting my money on a nice sunny day and a chance to dry out. What do you think?"

"That sun and clear sky could be deceptive. According to the radio there's another wave of this storm coming through."

"Uh, Jessica…" Dylan nervously cleared his throat then continued with what had been on his mind ever since he woke up that morning. "I know things have been a little strange around here. We got off to a bad start with the confusion over the use of the cabin, then it seems that everything kind of disintegrated through the morning and afternoon."

He saw the wariness in her eyes. "Why don't we call a truce to our misunderstandings…maybe take advantage of this sunny day and go for a walk in the woods? Getting out in the fresh air and indulging in a little exercise will probably do both of us some good." He extended a hesitant yet hopeful smile. "What do you say? Maybe some breakfast and then a nice walk?"

She paused a second before answering him, breathing a sigh of relief. He had thankfully refrained from mentioning the heated kisses they had shared. She had feared he would taunt her decision to put a stop to things…or worse yet, want to pick up where they had left off. It was a thought that gave her mixed feelings.

"Sure…" She returned his smile and tried to sound upbeat in agreeing with him that a truce was certainly in order. "That sounds like a good idea."

They made quick work of breakfast, dressed warmly, pulled on hiking boots, then set out from the cabin. The crisp morning air carried the scent of a mountain forest following a cleansing rain. The sunlight glistened off the still-wet needles of the Sitka spruce and Douglas fir. The silence was broken only by the cries of birds as they circled overhead, the occasional cone dropping from a fir tree and landing on the ground with a plop and the sounds of their own footsteps as they walked along the trail. They were each absorbed in private thoughts.

It was finally Dylan who made the first attempt at conversation. "It's been a long time since I was on the Olympic Peninsula. I'd forgotten what a beautiful place this is...." He stopped walking and took in a deep breath, then slowly expelled it. He stood still, moving only his head as his gaze swept over the scenery. "Fresh air, peaceful surroundings...it's very restful."

Jessica, too, stopped walking. "That's one of the reasons Justin and I settled on this location when we started looking for a getaway cabin. We ended up paying more money than we had planned on, but we fell in love with this particular area and couldn't resist the cabin. It's larger than what we had originally started looking for, but we're glad we went ahead with the deal."

"When did you buy it? The first I remember Justin mentioning it was a couple of years ago."

"We bought it four years ago. Sometimes it's a little difficult getting here in winter because of the snow." She looked around as the calm settled over her, a slight smile of contentment tugging at the corners of her mouth. "But it's worth the effort. I feel more relaxed here than anywhere I've ever been." She closed her eyes and turned her face toward the morning sun filtering through the trees.

Dylan studied her finely sculpted features and the way the sunlight caught the golden highlights of her hair. It was hard to believe that this enticingly stunning woman was that same teenager he had first met so many years ago. He drew a deep breath, in an attempt to counter the tightness that banded across his chest again.

"Do you get up here very often?" It was a stupid question, but he needed to say something to help break the tension building inside him.

"Not as often as I'd like. Probably once a month on the average for me and about the same for Justin. Our schedules very seldom coincide to let us be here at the same time."

"Do you ever rent the cabin out as a vacation place?"

"No. We talked about it but decided against it. We didn't want to be shut out of our own cabin if either of us had a last-minute cancellation of work and could get away for a couple of days." She shot him a side-long glance of disapproval, more in an effort to provide herself some emotional distance from him than anything else. She resumed walking along the trail. "Like when my New York project was postponed and I had a last-minute opportunity to use the cabin for a few days…what I thought would be a quiet getaway."

He continued down the trail walking along beside her. He spoke reflectively, almost as if he were talking to himself. "And I was there first, ruining all your plans and spoiling your quiet time."

She stopped walking again and turned to him, her eyes wide with surprise at what he had said. "That's not what I meant—"

He quickly pulled himself together. "Of course

not." He smiled condescendingly, making no effort to hide his feelings. "Don't worry, you've already explained the *rules* to me…you have no intention of being gracious and you have no desire to entertain guests."

She felt the sting of his pointed barb. "That's not fair. You're putting words in my mouth—"

"They were your words, not mine."

She looked up at him, her expression almost pleading for an end to what appeared to be the start of an argument. "But you've twisted the meaning. I only meant—"

His mouth was on hers before she could finish her sentence. He folded her into his arms. A little shiver darted across his nape when her fingers raked through his hair. Then he felt her arms slip around his neck. Every heated spark from the previous night came rushing back to him. He pulled her body so tightly against his that he literally lifted her off the ground. She was everything he could ever want, but he didn't know what to do about it. And the notion frightened him.

He reluctantly released her from his embrace, but continued to clasp her hand in his. He spoke softly, trying to keep his emotions under control. "It's too nice a day to spend it at odds with each other." He lifted his other hand and lightly traced the outline of her lips with the tip of his finger. "Don't you agree?"

"You're right." A shiver darted through her body. Her breathless reply matched his. "It's too nice a day."

He kept her hand firmly in his as they walked along the forest trail. The warmth of her touch radiated up his arm and through his body. His tension began to drain away, leaving only a sensation of well-being and contentment.

"You never did tell me how you got involved in public relations. Was that your area of study in college?"

"Yes. I had hoped to take a position with a large corporation after graduation, but it didn't work out the way I had planned."

"What happened?"

She paused a moment, a frown wrinkling her forehead. "I guess you could say marriage happened, and everything I wanted got put on hold for the duration."

"You mean your husband didn't want you to pursue a career?" He tried to suppress the laugh, but wasn't totally successful. "From what I've seen, I can't imagine you allowing someone else to control your life so completely."

She angrily jerked her hand out of his grasp, turned and glared at him. "And what's that supposed to mean? Just what is it you find so amusing?"

He stared blankly at her. "I didn't mean anything by it. It was just an observation."

Seeing the bewilderment in his eyes, she took a calming breath. "I'm sorry. I guess that's sort of a touchy subject with me."

"From what you've said…first his not wanting a family and now his not wanting you to pursue any interests of your own…it sounds like the two of you had some serious problems to work out."

"Well, let's just say that my marriage to him is a major regret in my life—one of those things I'd do differently if I had a chance to do it over again." She looked at Dylan for a moment as she turned a thought over in her mind.

"How about you? Is there anything in your life you'd do differently if you had the chance?" It was a loaded question, and she knew it. The way he had been protecting his reasons for being at the cabin told her there was something important bothering him. Every now and then she had gotten a quick glimpse of something beneath his smooth charm. It was enough to tell her that he had a layer of vulnerability which he kept carefully hidden. She wanted to know that level.

Justin was always telling her that she judged people too quickly and sometimes too harshly. Perhaps her brother had been right. She had predetermined that Dylan was the same type of man as her ex-husband. Possibly…just possibly…she had allowed her bad experience with marriage and the hurt that should have been relegated to the past to intrude on her impartial assessment of what was going on now. Or was she still trying to rationalize her very real attraction to Dylan Russell?

He looked away from her, preferring to focus his gaze on the landscape. Was there something he'd do differently? It was a list so long he didn't even know where to begin. He cautiously responded to her question, carefully choosing his words. "I imagine everyone has something they'd do differently if they had a second chance at it."

To his chagrin she persisted in her questioning. "What event in your life would you choose if you could do it over?"

"There are probably several things I'd elect to do differently if I had the opportunity." He laughed nervously, anxious to turn the focus of their conversation back on her. "What about your marriage…would you have handled it differently with the same man, chosen a different man or not gotten married at all? You said you wanted a family, so I imagine that would preclude your staying single.''

She wrinkled her brow into a frown. ''They say hindsight is twenty-twenty. In retrospect I wouldn't have entered into a marriage without first finding out what he wanted from the relationship, and I would have told him what I wanted.'' An edge of anger crept into her voice. ''We would have discussed important issues such as children and careers.''

She stared at him for a long moment before continuing. An uncomfortable level of anxiety began to build inside him. ''In short, I'd make sure he was looking for a marriage that was an equal partnership, each having respect for the other's opinions and goals.''

He saw the pain in her eyes, a hurt she obviously hadn't been able to hide and issues she hadn't totally reconciled yet. It touched that vulnerable spot deep inside him, the one he had tried to protect from an emotional assault. He brought her hand to his lips, kissed her palm, then held her hand against his chest. His words were barely above a whisper. ''I'm sorry things didn't work out for you.''

He felt so close to her at that moment and for the first time in more years than he could remember he wanted to share something deeply personal with someone else. He wanted to share it with Jessica. A thousand butterflies instantly materialized in his stomach, each battling for its own space. A tremor of panic started deep inside him and quickly spread through his body.

He opened his mouth and the words tumbled out. ''I once came within minutes—literally—of getting

The Editor's "Thank You" Free Gifts Include:

● Two BRAND-NEW romance novels!
● An exciting mystery gift!

PLACE
FREE GIFT
SEAL
HERE

YES! I have placed my Editor's "Thank You" seal in the space provided above. Please send me 2 free books and a fabulous mystery gift. I understand I am under no obligation to purchase any books, as explained on the back and on the opposite page.

326 SDL DCQE

225 SDL DCP9
(S-D-OS-03/01)

NAME   (PLEASE PRINT CLEARLY)

ADDRESS

APT.#   CITY

STATE/PROV.   ZIP/POSTAL CODE

Thank You!

The Silhouette Reader Service™ — Here's how it works:

married.'' He chuckled nervously in an attempt to cover his anxiety. "I was sort of left at the altar.''

She blurted out her surprise. "Really? Someone jilted *you?* It doesn't seem—'' The crimson color spread across her cheeks and forehead as she glanced down for a moment before looking up at him again. "I'm sorry. I didn't mean that the way it sounded. It's just that, well, I've never thought of you as the type to ever get married. And I can't imagine someone walking out on you....''

He took in a calming breath. "I guess we all have things in our pasts that would come as a surprise to others.''

"Uh, what happened, if you don't mind my asking.''

"It seems that she was only using me to force some rich married man thirty years her senior to divorce his wife and marry her. She had me completely fooled as she played her little game. She pushed for us to get married right away, and I went along with it. There weren't any formal preparations, just a simple justice of the peace ceremony. It was a last-minute whirlwind decision prompted by what was supposed to be *love*.'' He made no attempt to control the sarcasm and bitterness that forced its way to the surface. "The *other man* showed up and told her she had won...he had left his wife. That was the last time I saw her.''

Jessica reached out and touched his arm as a gesture of comfort and understanding. "I'm sorry. I didn't know. Justin never mentioned it to me.''

"I'm not sure he even knows. It's not something I like to talk about.'' Or to be even more accurate, it was something he never talked about, just as he had never told anyone about what happened with the

Clarksons. A blanket of despair settled over him. He tried to shake it away, but became lost in his own thoughts, momentarily oblivious to what was going on around him.

A sudden wave of sadness and loneliness washed over Jessica when she saw the expression on his face. It was as if she had tapped in to his emotions. She had wanted to see beneath that smooth, perfect outer shell of Dylan Russell, but now that she had gained a glimpse of the inner person she wasn't so sure she wanted to know any more. It certainly explained where his cynical attitude toward marriage had come from. An overwhelming need filled her with a desire to say something. She wanted to let him know she understood the pain of a failed relationship, even though she couldn't possibly fully comprehend the extent of the impact caused by the way he had been used and dumped or the type of pain he still carried around because of it.

She ventured a tentative question, not sure of her ground or how much she had the right to ask. "Is that why you wanted to use the cabin? To kind of pull yourself together after…well, after your—"

Her question brought his attention back to the present. A bittersweet laugh escaped his throat. "No. My close brush with that *unnatural* state known as marriage was many years ago, right after I graduated from college."

"'Unnatural state'? I see you haven't let your experience stop you from keeping an open mind."

He cocked his head, arched an eyebrow and leveled a steady gaze at her. "And what about you? You've been divorced for several years and have apparently chosen to devote your time and energy to work rather than a personal life, even though you indicated that you wanted to have children.''

"Well…" Her defenses leaped into play. ''That's entirely different. I've been building a career. I haven't had time to think about—'' Her words came to an abrupt halt when she saw the teasing glint come into his eyes. An inner sigh of relief caught her by surprise. It was almost as if she was glad that he had apparently snapped out of his momentary despair. It had pained her to see him so despondent, although she wasn't sure exactly why.

"'Entirely different'? I suppose you could rationalize it that way if you wanted to.''

He clasped her hand in his and started walking again. She welcomed the warmth of his touch. He had already shown a depth she never realized he possessed. There was a lot more to Dylan Russell than she had suspected. And she wanted to know it all. Was she repeating old patterns and falling under the spell of a charming scoundrel? If so, she was willingly allowing him to lead her on.

Six

Jessica tried to keep the conversation going, torn between wanting to know everything about Dylan and not wanting to step all over his feelings. "Is that, uh, is that why you decided to become a con man?"

He came to an abrupt halt, released her hand and turned until he fully faced her. "A con man?"

She saw a strange combination of surprise and hurt flicker across his features. She regretted her bad choice of words. "I mean your business deals. Justin always referred to them as high-flying wheeler-dealer speculation. I just assumed that—"

He heaved an audible sigh. It was almost as if he had resigned himself to having to comply with an unreasonable request. "You certainly have some strange notions about who and what I am. Justin would say that to me, too, but it was always said as a joke."

Her embarrassment inserted itself into her voice. "I

seem to be putting my foot farther into my mouth each time I say something. I guess it's just that…well…" Her gaze connected with his and held there for a long moment. Her pulse raced a little harder and her heart beat a little faster. "You've always been a kind of larger-than-life mystery—a globe-trotting playboy whose every action was unconventional, compared to my life. And Justin is always telling tales about your latest adventures. I assumed they were true. And, uh, I just never could get a clear picture about you."

Another bittersweet chuckle was his immediate response to her revelations. Is this what his life had been reduced to? Speculation about his honesty? "Then I suppose I should straighten you out on a few things. You don't mind if we walk at the same time, do you? I seem to have a lot of pent-up energy that I need to work off."

Dylan started down the trail again without waiting for an answer from Jessica. She stayed close at his side. He stuck his hands in his jacket pockets and furrowed his brow in concentration as he sorted things out in his mind. "I guess I should start with college. I graduated with a degree in finance and had just gone to work for a very prestigious stock brokerage firm. A little less than three months later my fiancée jilted me, then two weeks after that my mother died. I tried very hard to work within the parameters of the job requirements, but each passing day became more difficult. I couldn't put the restlessness aside or stick with the rigid atmosphere and rules of the brokerage house. I finally ended up resigning from the firm.

"That's when I sort of fell into my first big deal, and I was hooked almost like an adrenaline surge. I had found my calling. Everything took off like a rocket—world travel, first-class lifestyle and lots of glamour. I thought I had it all.''

Another wave of melancholy assaulted his consciousness. He stopped walking and stared at her for a moment. ''Then a few months ago something happened…and—'' he glanced across the horizon as he tried to collect his thoughts ''—it all fell apart for me. I finally made my way to what I thought would be a good place to figure what to do with my life. I ended up here.''

''So that's why you're here? To make plans for the future?''

''Something like that. I also have some, uh, well…*personal* problems to work out—some fallout from the last deal I put together.''

''What happened? Is there anything I can help with?''

He shook his head, not sure how to respond to her questions. ''One of my projects went bad. None of my deals were ever scams or con jobs. I never knowingly participated in anything illegal or unethical. My business deals were speculative high-risk venture capital. Big risk hopefully resulting in big gain. I always carefully explained all the pitfalls and risks to all prospective investors.'' A moment of reflection crept into his words. ''I thought I was dealing only with people who could afford the loss if the risk didn't pan out.''

He continued walking again. ''That's not to say that there aren't a lot of con men involved in the same type of activity. I've certainly seen my share of them—the leeches who prey on the unsuspecting—but I wasn't one of them.''

He thought of Rose and Stanley Clarkson again. His voice dropped to a barely audible whisper, and a hint of despair returned. "Of course, sometimes things go wrong…. A deal can fall apart, and everyone loses their money without it being the result of any wrong-doing or anyone's fault."

"Is that what happened? You lost a lot of money?"

"Me? No, it wasn't as simple as that. I didn't lose any money. If it had just been me it wouldn't have mattered." He swallowed down the emotion that choked in his throat. He couldn't say any more. He wasn't ready to talk about the Clarksons. He'd already said far more than he had intended.

They walked along in silence again. He thought about his plan for the future. Even more pieces than he had fit together the previous night were coming together in his mind. What had been total chaos two days ago was now forming into a workable plan. It was as if being able to talk about what was going on inside him had helped make things clearer in his mind. And the person he had been able to talk to had been Jessica. A comfortable warmth settled over him, pro-viding a surprising feeling of closeness.

Jessica again captured his attention when she linked her arm through his at the elbow. He liked the sen-sation the personal gesture conveyed. For three months he had been wrestling with the problem of what to do with his life. It had been a time of confusion and brutal introspection about who and what he had become. And now, less than forty-eight hours after waking up to find Jessica McGuire in bed with him, he had pulled those pieces of confusion together into the framework of a workable plan.

Could she have been the cause? The spark that set the wheels in motion? He wasn't sure, but if it was true, then he was well on his way to a very sincere emotional involvement...something he swore he'd never allow to happen again. He was definitely in over his head, but had he been thrown an anchor that would weigh him down or a life preserver to keep him afloat? A little tremor ran up his back. Perhaps she was both...the anchor that would keep him grounded in reality while at the same time being the life preserver that rescued him from his inner turmoil.

He had never thought in depth about emotional matters before, never analyzed anything beyond the dollars and cents of the business deal he was working on. A wave of apprehension splashed through his consciousness leaving him a little uneasy. She was the type who made a man think about what could be, to strive for better things. Another tremor rippled through his body accompanied by an equal dose of panic.

They walked along the trail in silence for a while. Conversation began slowly and stayed superficial as they talked about nature, the scenery, weather, movies and books...safe topics that didn't require either of them to delve into painful areas or confront buried fears. They settled into a comfortable mode as they held hands and talked about likes and dislikes, favorite foods and generally got to know a little about each other.

Dylan laced their fingers together. He liked the feel of her hand in his. It had a calming effect on the uncertainty that had plagued him for the past few months. It gave him a sense of purpose, along with an overwhelming desire to seek her approval. He had never before been concerned with having someone else's approval. He had always known who he was, what he was doing and where he was going...until three months ago.

He stopped walking, pulled her into his arms and captured her mouth with a kiss that radiated part physical desire and part deep emotion. He wanted to know her more than he had ever wanted to know anyone.

Jessica bounded up the steps to the porch and plopped down on the bench next to the door. "I'm starved. I think I could eat the contents of an entire grocery store." She pulled off a muddy boot.

Dylan's spontaneous laugh filled the air. "If you deplete the world's food supply that sure doesn't leave anything for me, does it?"

He knelt in front of her, motioning for her to extend her other leg. "Here...let me do that." He pulled off her other boot and dropped it on the porch.

Their long walk had produced a day of carefree ease, a time of sharing personal feelings and even tentatively allowing some inner fears to show. It had been an exhilarating experience that brought them closer together. Hand holding and casual kisses had led to some decidedly heated kisses. There was a definite chemistry working between them that neither could deny. And they still had the entire evening and night.

She leaned back against the wall and closed her eyes. A slight smile turned the corners of her mouth. "We've been walking for hours. It sure feels good to sit down."

He studied her a moment. Her delicately sculpted features tugged at his senses, and her very kissable mouth sent a rush of excitement through his body. He leaned forward and brushed his lips against hers hoping it would satisfy the urge to sweep her into his arms again and this time carry her upstairs, but all it did was whet his appetite for more. He tugged at her hand, pulling her up from the bench. A moment later he folded her in his embrace and brought his mouth down fully on hers.

The moment his lips touched hers all she could think about was how much he excited her, how much she wanted to be part of his life. She allowed the delicious kiss to continue for several seconds. Once again being in his arms transported her beyond the concerns and fears of what might be. He stirred more in her than sensual desires. Oddly enough, he also made her feel protected and cared for. It wasn't logical, certainly didn't make any sense, but she could not deny the truth of it.

She broke off the kiss, but her breathless voice gave away the emotional depth of her involvement. There was more going on than her physical response to his action. She looked up into his eyes and saw the same things she was feeling...or perhaps it was just wishful thinking. Another wave of desire swept through her. She took a couple of steps away from his touch, hoping to break the pull his magnetism exerted on her.

"I...I think I'd better see what there is to fix for—" she glanced at her watch "—well, it's definitely too late for lunch, and it's a little early for dinner."

He reached out and grabbed her hand. "I'm hungry, too."

The look in his eyes said he was hungry for more than food. A little shiver of trepidation raced up her spine. Was it a portent of what the evening would bring? The level of excitement rose, only to be tempered with caution. Her gaze locked with his. Neither of them moved. She rubbed her hand across her nape to still the shiver, then pulled away.

"Whatever we have for dinner, it might have to

come out of a can. Do you prefer chunky thick vegetable soup or beef stew?''

He took a calming breath as he attempted to cool off his heated desires. He held the door open for her and flashed a casual smile. ''Why don't you surprise me?''

They went directly to the kitchen. She opened a cupboard and peered inside. ''I see some pasta that I can cook and serve with canned marinara sauce.'' She moved a few things around. ''We also have some backpacker's meals...ham with green beans and scalloped potatoes or chicken with sliced carrots and rice pilaf. It's amazing what you can buy nowadays that doesn't need to be refrigerated. And it tastes surprisingly good, too.''

He pulled her into his arms. ''That's not the only thing around here that tastes good.'' He nibbled on her ear, then slid his lips around to her mouth. It was a brief kiss, but one filled with the promise of things to come. His gaze lingered on her mouth, then captured her gaze and held it for several seconds.

He stepped back from her as he took a deep breath in hopes of breaking the now-familiar tightness across his chest. Even though the afternoon had ended up being a carefree time devoid of tension, he still carried the memory of her comments about him being a con man and all the unsavory associations that went with it.

He brushed a quick kiss across her lips. ''I intend to change your initial impression of me.''

''My first impression?'' She flashed a teasing grin. ''You mean back when I was fifteen years old?''

He cocked his head, his amusement spreading

across his features. "Fifteen? I think we can safely say we've moved past that."

Her initial opinion of the type of man he was had already changed drastically from her preconceived notions of the man she found in her bed. The part of him he had shared during the course of the day had shown her a man with much more substance than she had at first believed him to have. Yes, her original judgment of him had definitely changed, but exactly how did she feel about him now? She knew more about him than she had, yet she suspected there was a great deal more that she didn't know.

And she wanted to know it all.

He glanced toward the fireplace, then the front porch before returning his attention to her. "The firewood supply is getting very low…at least the smaller pieces. I'll build a fire, then split some of those larger logs into a usable size."

"While you're doing that, I'll get some food on the table."

He took her hand and gave it a squeeze, sending a surge of warmth through her body, then headed for the porch to bring in the last of the kindling. As soon as he had a nice fire going he grabbed the ax and headed for the porch.

A few minutes later, drawn by the chopping sounds, she wandered to the front window. Her hunger pangs faded away as she watched him work. He had taken off his sweater, leaving just his T-shirt. She watched him as he methodically placed the somewhat unwieldy logs on end and split them in two lengthwise, then in turn split each of the halves lengthwise again.

The taut muscle tone of his arms and back could not be hidden by his T-shirt. The image of his well-defined chest and his broad shoulders had continued to linger in her mind from that first morning, but she hadn't realized just how strong he was until she saw him split the logs with one powerful overhead swing of the ax.

Once again he had surprised her. Chopping firewood was not something an international playboy would be doing. It was not the type of activity she would have associated with him, or at least with the type of person she thought he was. He was doing a good job of refuting who and what she had always believed of him. She continued to watch him for a moment longer. It helped her understand who he wasn't, but it didn't tell her anything about who he was.

She stepped out on the porch as he stacked the last piece of wood by the door. She gestured toward the results of his hard work while extending a teasing smile. "I must say I'm very impressed. You seem to be experienced in chopping wood."

He grabbed her arm, pulled her body against his and returned her teasing grin. "I told you I'd change your first impression of me, and this is only the beginning." He grabbed his sweater from the porch railing, then escorted her into the cabin.

"I worked up quite an appetite with all that hard work. So...what's to eat? I need to keep up my strength, you know. Never can tell when I'll need that little extra bit of energy." He gave her a sly wink, then headed for the dining table.

They ate quickly, then carried their wineglasses to the large floor pillows in front of the fireplace. They talked quietly while sipping their wine and enjoying the sensual warmth of the fire. The relaxed atmosphere allowed them to each finally let down the protective guard that had never completely been dismissed. The conversation eventually turned to Dylan's plans for the future.

Where he had been hesitant that afternoon, he now wanted to share the idea that he had been formulating in his mind. He wanted to know her thoughts and feelings about his plan.

He nervously cleared his throat. "Would you mind if I bounced an idea off you?" He pulled her into his arms and leaned back against the pillows. The tension shot through his body. Was he about to make a huge mistake? He had taken a chance when he shared the information about his almost marriage. But that had been something from his past. These plans were now, they had a definite impact on his entire future.

"Of course not." She snuggled into the comfort of his embrace.

He paused to gather his thoughts before he went the final step in laying bare his guarded inner self. "As I told you, I wanted the use of the cabin to think out what I needed as a new direction for my life. This is what I've come up with." An anxious tremor coursed through his body before finally subsiding. "Tell me what you think."

He took a calming breath then plunged in headfirst. "I want to start a business, actually a service of sorts, for people who have been taken in by financial scams. I don't have all the details worked out yet, but it's pretty much set in my mind." The plan had grown and the pieces fused together in direct proportion to his growing involvement with Jessica. Intellectually he knew it was true, but to know it emotionally was a different matter. He tried to shake off that reality as he started to explain his plan.

"I envision it as a sort of seminar where they can get their financial life put back together, learn how to manage their money and rebuild for the future. It would also include information about how to recognize scams and con jobs. The seminar could be presented through the local chamber of commerce, by various civic organizations or as adult education night school. There are several possibilities. It would be a nonprofit endeavor. Any fee charged for the service would be minimal and only for the purposes of covering out-of-pocket expenses for the sponsoring organization, things like rental of the space to hold the class if that's necessary."

Another jitter of anxiety darted through his body. He searched her expression for any hint of her thoughts. Once again he found himself seeking her approval and unsure of what her response would be. He tried to set aside his apprehension, but couldn't keep the hint of hopefulness out of his voice. "Well? What do you think?"

She studied the expectant look on his face, the uncertainty in his eyes. "What do I think?" An emotional wave flowed through her, accompanied by a tender feeling of caring and pride. Her words came out in a hushed awe. "I think that sounds wonderful. I'm truly impressed."

The sigh of relief reverberated inside him. It was almost as if he'd been holding his breath waiting for her to say something. He pulled her body tighter against his, wrapping her completely within his embrace. "I'm...well...I'm a little nervous about it. A project like this will take a long-term commitment on my part. That's something I've been worried about…just like Justin with his purchase of the charter company. I need to be sure this is the right thing for me to be doing. I don't want to start something that involves other people, then find out it isn't what I thought it would be. I have to consider the consequences of my actions and what the impact of those actions will be on others.''

He had just shared something with Jessica that he had never mentioned to anyone else, something he had not even clearly formulated into exact words. He had told her of his concerns about consequences, concerns brought on by his previous actions. It had been a difficult decision. It had required that he adopt a whole new way of thinking about the future. Thoughts of the Clarksons again filled his mind, strengthening his resolve to follow through with his plans and accomplish something worthwhile.

He ran his fingers through her hair as he cradled her head against his shoulder. That moment…stretched out in front of the fire with Jessica in his arms…filled him with a sense of contentment that he hadn't felt in many years. She was the most extraordinary woman he had ever met, someone who touched his very soul the way no one else ever had.

His contented frame of mind didn't last long as troubling thoughts and fears seeped into his consciousness. Making a commitment to start his finance seminar was a big enough step in its own right. Could he cope with a leap into the emotional sea at the same time? Did he have the courage to allow the possibility? He didn't know. His usual confidence had deserted him, leaving him uncertain and unsure of what to do.

He tried to shove the uncomfortable feelings aside.

He didn't want to dwell on the problems. All he wanted for that evening was to be with Jessica, to enjoy the time they had together. The emotional magnitude of the moment washed over him. He shifted his weight until he was able to lean across her body as it nestled into the floor pillows. He captured her mouth with a kiss, igniting the passion that had been smoldering deep inside him. He caressed her shoulders, ran his hand along her rib cage, then around the curve of her hip. He rolled over on his side, taking her with him.

Jessica had never felt as close to anyone as she did to Dylan at that moment. She knew she had finally gotten through that devil-may-care outer shell of the globe-trotting bon vivant to find the substance of the real man. He was so much more than the superficial playboy she had always assumed him to be. She certainly understood how he could charm his way into whatever he wanted, because he had clearly charmed his way into her heart.

His sensual touch set off a chain reaction of sensations ranging from a physical craving for his touch to an emotional connection she couldn't even describe. Her breath caught in her throat. A surge of excitement raced through her body. A sense of reckless abandon took hold of her, the thrill of an illicit encounter with a dangerous man. The stimulating reality produced an out-of-control intensity that frightened her orderly sense of things. Then any thought she might have had about putting a stop to what was happening disappeared in a heartbeat when he ran his tongue across her lower lip before invading the dark recesses of her mouth.

She pressed her body against his, boldly skimming

her fingers across his bare skin beneath the back of his sweater. Everything his earlier kisses had promised now proved to be true. There was no doubt in her mind that they would end up making love before the night was over, even though she suspected it would be the worst possible decision she could make. Just the thought of it sent a heated wave coursing through her body. She reveled in the sensations as the texture of his tongue scraped against hers. Her breathing became more labored as her excitement grew.

His arousal strained at the confines of his jeans. He drew away from her mouth, exchanging her addictive taste for the creamy smoothness of her skin. He nibbled at the corner of her mouth, kissed his way across her cheek and down the side of her neck. All logical thought deserted him. Any honorable intentions he might have harbored went up in smoke.

He pushed up her sweater and deftly unhooked her bra. Her tautly puckered nipple pressed into his palm as he cupped her breast. He took the other nipple into his mouth, his tongue teasing the pebbled texture of the bud. Her soft moan radiated pure pleasure and fired his ardor. A surge of excitement coursed through his body.

A hard jolt of anxiety hit him, quickly replacing the exhilaration. He released the treat from his mouth. He hadn't experienced this type of nervousness since his college days. He didn't know anything about her type of woman—if he was rushing her, what her needs might be, whether he would be able to satisfy them. He brought his mouth down on hers with an added fervor in an attempt to shake away the doubts. Her sensual stroking of his back sent a rush through his body, giving added impetus to his desires. He held her tighter, every nerve ending wanting her.

He grabbed the bottom of her sweater. His words came out thick, attesting to his state of arousal. "Let's get rid of this." He tugged at the sweater but only succeeded in getting it caught on her bra hooks. He struggled with the tangled mess. They both tried, but even with her assistance the garments refused to co-operate and only became more tangled.

"Damn!" Dylan inhaled a ragged breath in an effort to calm his growing frustration. The situation looked more like a disaster in the making than a smooth seduction or an enticing prelude to lovemaking. Was this how the evening would end? Like a scene from a slapstick comedy?

Jessica gasped for air. Her frustration matched his. Her unfastened bra and sweater were hopelessly twisted together to the point where her erratic movements had only made things worse. She closed her eyes and took another deep breath as a tremor ran through her body.

"Jessica…" He couldn't make the words come out. His husky voice conveyed his lack of total control. He felt her tremble as he held her in his arms. He framed her face with his hands and allowed his gaze to wander across her face—her kiss-swollen lips, the slight flush across her cheeks and the passion that sparkled in her eyes. He had never felt so inadequate as he had for the past few minutes. He wanted her. He wanted to intimately know every physical inch of her body and every emotional moment of her soul.

He didn't want to play games with her. She deserved better. She deserved honesty. He gently brushed his lips against hers. "Jessica…I want very much to make love to you. I want to do it right, not like this…not like two teenagers groping in the back seat of a car.''

He stood up and held out his hand to her. ''Come upstairs with me?'' He felt as if he were in a win or lose situation where the stakes were very high and the consequences all important. She was not just another woman and this was not a simple one-night stand or quick affair. An uneasy tremor of apprehension darted through him as he held his breath and waited for her to answer.

Conflicting thoughts and feelings tore her in two directions. The woman who had been mesmerized by his charm, inflamed by his kisses and who burned with desire for his touch wanted to go with him…no questions asked and no promises required. However, the sensible, logical, feet-on-the-ground independent woman knew the pitfalls of giving in to those desires. She had been down that path before. She looked up into his eyes and saw only honesty and caring. She placed her hand in his and stood up. Would she end up regretting her decision? Possibly so, but for tonight nothing else mattered except being with Dylan Russell.

He grabbed one of the oil lamps, lit it and carried it with him as they walked upstairs hand in hand. She paused when they reached her bedroom door and gestured toward the other bedroom. ''I believe Justin has some, uh…''

''I know. I saw them when I was looking for something to read last night.'' He gave her hand a squeeze as he leaned forward and placed a soft kiss on her lips. ''I'll be right back.''

Seven

Jessica untangled her bra from her sweater and dumped both of them on the chair next to the bed. She unfastened her jeans and was about to remove them when the light from the oil lamp invaded the nearly dark room. She turned toward Dylan. Her heartbeat jumped. He wore only his briefs. The illumination highlighted his handsome features, the well-defined planes of his chest and his long, muscular legs. A tremor of anticipation darted up her spine and swirled around inside her.

He set the lamp on the nightstand along with the packets he had taken from Justin's nightstand. He turned down the wick until only a soft glow remained. Even in the dim light she could see the passion and excitement in his eyes. He placed his hands on her shoulders, then lightly trailed his fingers down her arms.

"Are you sure about this, Jessica?" He couldn't still the quaver in his voice or the nervous jitter that attacked his insides. He had never wanted anyone as much as he wanted her. "I don't want you to feel like you were being unfairly coerced or—"

"I'm very sure."

In fact, she had never been so sure of anything in her entire life as she was at that moment. His hands ran up her rib cage, coming to rest just below her breasts. Little shivers of excitement rippled across her skin in the wake of his touch. An intoxicating fervor assailed her senses, pushing her desires beyond anything she had ever experienced to a whole new level.

He sat on the edge of the bed, his gaze slowly drinking her in—the sparkle in her eyes, her slightly parted lips, the firm curve of her breasts. A low moan escaped his throat as he kissed each of her puckered nipples. He couldn't stop the huskiness that clung to his words. "You are absolutely exquisite."

Dylan ran the tip of his tongue from the base of her throat down to the valley between her breasts while tugging her jeans past her hips to the floor. She stepped out of them, shoving them aside with her foot. He drew her nipple into his mouth and gently suckled while caressing her back. His fingers ran across her bare skin moving lower and lower. He eased one hand inside her panties and cupped the roundness of her bottom. A moment later he slid the panties down her legs to the floor.

He placed a soft kiss between her breasts, then captured her other nipple and held it in his mouth. He savored the texture with his tongue, the experience enhanced when she wrapped her arms around his neck and ran her fingers through his hair. A low moan of pleasure filled the air. He thought it was his, but it felt as if it came from her. Either way, he knew what was about to happen would be something very special because Jessica was very special.

He fell backward onto the bed taking her with him, holding her body tightly on top of his. The warmth of his skin heated her desires. Once again his tongue ran along the edge of her lower lip, then brushed against hers. The moan of delight caught in her throat. Her entire body tingled with excitement. She responded fully and without reservation to each and every tantalizing sensation he created.

She tugged at his briefs, desperately wanting them out of the way. She had never been so brazen, so aggressive, especially with someone who was still a stranger to her in many ways. His hand brushed against hers when he arched his hips up from the bed and accomplished what she had been attempting. He yanked away the last remaining physical barrier between them.

Bare skin pressed against bare skin along the length of their bodies. Their combined intensity filled the room with a heightened degree of sensual electricity. They had an entire night ahead of them in which to indulge their desires, yet each seemed consumed by a nearly out-of-control urgency.

Dylan again captured her mouth with an all-consuming kiss that left nothing hidden. He skimmed his hands along the length of her torso then tickled his fingers across the sensitive skin of her inner thigh drawing ever closer to the core of her sexual being. Every contact enhanced his already-overstimulated desire for her. He brushed his fingers through the downy softness between her thighs then penetrated her moist heat.

A wave of ecstasy shot through Jessica's body. She arched her hips toward his hand, the intimate physical contact sending a swirl of euphoria around her, blotting out everything except the deep physical pleasure building inside her. She ran her hand along his thigh, then stroked his hardened arousal. She felt the low growl in his chest as much as heard it. Her ragged breathing came in hard gasps as the sensations built, layer upon layer.

As much as he wanted to savor each and every sensation—her gentle yet insistent touch as she stroked his manhood, her unbridled response to his ministrations—he knew his faltering control would not allow it. No one had ever excited him to the level where she did. He reached to the nightstand for one of the packets and quickly secured the condom.

Dylan rolled her over onto her back, then settled his body over hers. He gently probed at the entrance of her womanhood, then froze as a hard tremor of panic hit him. He had never been plagued by doubts before, but this time the emotional magnitude of what was about to happen pulled hard at his reality. He recaptured her mouth, as much to drive away his fears as to revel in the pleasure of her taste.

He thrust forward, completing the tangible connection between them. The moment her feminine folds closed around his hardness was the moment he *knew* something very profound had happened, but something he couldn't quite define. It scared him as much as it excited him. He set a smooth rhythm, immediately losing himself in the pure physical pleasure of their coupling.

Jessica arched her hips to meet each of his down-ward strokes. He filled her both physically and emo-tionally, erasing her few remaining concerns about whether she was doing the right thing. Nothing had ever felt so right in her entire life. And no one had ever touched her soul as deeply as he did.

They moved together in harmony, their pace esca-lating with each stroke until the convulsions claimed her in an all-consuming burst of rapture. She threw her head back into the pillow, breaking the intensity of the kiss. She gasped for air. The waves of euphoria washed over her as her arms and legs wrapped tightly around his body.

Dylan had reached the limit of his tenuous control when her fulfillment resonated to him. He gave one final deep plunge. The hard spasms shuddered through his body. He held her tightly in his arms and buried his face in her hair, desperate to make sure any errant thoughts would not be verbalized. He did not want to say what he was feeling, did not want to acknowledge just how emotionally involved he had become with Jessica McGuire.

He gulped in a lungful of air as the spasms subsided. He brushed a loose tendril of hair away from her damp cheek, replacing it with a soft kiss. He continued to hold her in his arms while trying to bring control to his ragged breathing. He had never had anything hit him quite as hard as the implications of having made love with Jessica. He had suffered a quick bout of anxiety earlier, but now it had become full-blown panic. He closed his eyes and tried to calm his thoughts...and his fears.

Jessica snuggled into his embrace. She had never experienced anything like Dylan Russell. He made her heart sing and elevated her level of intensity to the point where it made a mockery of her orderly sense of things. He filled her with so much emotion that it truly frightened her. And intermingled with all of that was the word *love*. She wasn't sure where the word had come from or what to do about it, but she couldn't deny its existence.

He was the last person she should be having those thoughts about, but they refused to go away. Did she dare to hope that she would be able to erase his negative thoughts about a permanent relationship? That she could be the one to capture Dylan Russell's heart and keep it? Her euphoria became tempered by concerns and doubts. She chose to set aside everything except the here and now—the warmth, caring and protection he folded around her as he held her in his arms, gently stroking her skin and hair. She closed her eyes and allowed his sensual touch to lull her to sleep.

Her deep, even breathing accompanied the gentle rise and fall of her breasts. Never had anything affected him like making love with Jessica. She had literally turned his world inside out and left him grasping for explanations and reality. The strong emotions surging through his consciousness were unlike any he had ever experienced, including those he thought was love for his ex-fiancée. Did he dare consider the possibility of this being the start of a very deep and real love? The full-blown implications scared him to death.

The haunting fears that had lived inside him since the day he was left at the altar continued to plague him. And to that ongoing emotional burden had been added the trauma of his life seeming to unravel before his eyes. He looked at the sleeping Jessica, and his heart swelled with the deep feelings he had for her.

How many more changes in his life could he handle with everything being thrown at him at once? And more important, how could he expect anyone else to share that life when everything around him was so unsettled?

He kissed her on the forehead, then sank into the bed with his arms wrapped around her. He closed his eyes and tried to force the doubts and fears from his mind. Now he was even more troubled about his future than he had been when he arrived at the cabin. This time his concerns included Jessica McGuire and the role she would play in his life. A troubled sleep finally claimed him.

Dylan watched Jessica as she slept. The early-morning light filtered in through the bedroom windows, falling across her sleeping form. It highlighted the delicate features of her face and revealed the enticing curves of her body. Her long, dark lashes rested against her upper cheek, and her blond hair feathered softly over her forehead. A tightness pulled across his chest in conflict with the strong emotions that welled inside him. He had never seen anyone more beautiful or desirable in his life. A little tickle of panic stabbed at him telling him it was far more than merely physical desire that had captured his senses.

He glanced over to the nightstand, to the three empty condom packets. Two more times that night they had made love, each time more exciting than the previous—the most recent only three hours ago. And each time left him more fearful of where things were headed and how deeply he had already become involved with her. She filled that emptiness inside him, that place that had long cried out for something but he hadn't known what...until now.

He pressed his lips softly against her cheek. An involuntary sigh of contentment reverberated through his body, followed by a shiver of apprehension. He wrapped her in his arms and pulled her body against his, being careful not to wake her. The feel of her bare skin against his immediately renewed the desires that had been simmering just below the surface. If their night of lovemaking had done nothing else it had told him that he would never have enough of her, that he would always want more. She was like an intoxicating substance, and he was totally addicted.

An anxious tremor cut short his time of quiet reflection. He hadn't really given any thought to what she might be expecting from him. Would she assume a commitment for the future? It was a consideration he hadn't had to face before, not with the women he was accustomed to being with. They all knew what the score was, and it didn't include any type of commitment or promises. But Jessica...he didn't know what to expect with her. He wasn't sure exactly what he wanted, either. He knew what he didn't want. He did not want to lose her. He did not want their lives to take separate paths.

Jessica stirred awake, stretching her legs and arms while arching her back. His rapidly escalating desires pushed his concerns aside. He rolled her body over on top of his, tickled his fingertips lightly across her bare bottom, then settled her hips against his. Her soft moan, accompanied by a sexy smile, sent a wave of excitement rippling through his body. He nibbled tenderly on her earlobe, then at the corners of her mouth.

A low growl made its way out of his throat when she ran her foot along his calf.

The thick remnants of sleep clung to his voice. "Good morning." He brushed a soft kiss against her lips. "Did you have a good night's sleep?" He slid his hand to her inner thigh while extending a wry smile. "Do you feel well rested?"

"Mmm…" She moved her hips just enough to let him know she was fully aware of his arousal. "That's a leading question."

His whispered words tickled across her ear. "In case my lecherous intentions somehow eluded you…" He cupped the rounded globes of her buttocks and pulled her hips tightly against his as he captured her mouth with a quick yet sensual kiss.

"I don't think anything about you has eluded me." A shiver of desire told her how deeply his touch affected her. As much as the idea of making love again appealed to her, she tried to put forth a more logical and sensible agenda. "Don't you think we should be thinking about getting out of bed?"

He wrapped his arms around her, caressing her back and shoulders. He kissed her cheek, his manner and tone conveying his teasing intention. "Not me. I'd be content to stay right here all day…." His words trailed off as his expression turned serious. "As long as you agreed to stay here with me."

"That's a very tempting offer," she took a steadying breath in an attempt to calm her highly stimulated desires, "but I think we'd better check the weather conditions and see if we can get to the market for some groceries."

He kissed her tenderly on the lips. "I suppose you're right."

Each hurried to shower and dress. He made coffee while she fixed the last of the breakfast supplies he had brought with him. The news on the radio said the bridge had been reopened. It provided a sobering moment. They were no longer stranded, either of them could leave. As if having silently agreed in advance, neither of them mentioned that possibility. They made quick work of breakfast, then took her car and went to the market for supplies. By midmorning they had finished with all the necessities.

Dylan took her hand in his. "What would you say to a nice walk in the woods?"

"That sounds like a terrific idea."

They walked along the trail hand in hand, comfortable with the silence and content just to be together.

Jessica allowed her thoughts to wander to what it would be like to live with the excitement of Dylan Russell as a permanent part of her life—to wake up each morning with him at her side and go to bed each night wrapped in his arms. What she felt was far more than just physical attraction…she was beginning to believe it really was love.

She managed to suppress the grin that tugged at the corners of her mouth when she thought about Justin finding his supply of condoms not as plentiful as they had been. She glanced up at Dylan and was about to share her amusement over the condoms when she noticed the pensive expression on his face.

A little tremor of apprehension darted through her body. Were the concerns she saw written across his features about her? About their night of making love? Another touch of panic pushed at her. Had she fallen into a trap from which there was no escape? Had she fallen in love with a man who would end up breaking her heart? She tried to shove the uneasy feelings aside, to return to the euphoria that had enveloped her when she woke that morning.

She squeezed his hand to get his attention. "You look like something's bothering you." She took a calming breath and asked the question she wasn't really sure she wanted an answer to. "Anything you'd like to share?"

He stopped walking and stared at her for a moment, not sure exactly how to respond to her question. He leaned down and placed a tender kiss on her lips. The thoughts had been circulating through his mind along with a growing need to be able to share his inner turmoil with someone. His words were hesitant at first. "Yes...I think I would like to share it with you."

Dylan sat on a large rock, scooting back to make room for Jessica to sit in front of him. He wrapped his arms around her, snuggling her into his body so that her back rested against his chest. He took a steadying breath to curb the anxiety growing inside him. It was a story he had thought he would never tell anyone, but he wanted Jessica to know what happened. He wanted her to know about Rose and Stanley Clarkson.

"This is very difficult for me to talk about, so please bear with me." He rested his cheek against the top of her head. "It all started about a year ago." A little shiver of anxiety darted down his spine. "I was in London. I had just closed a very tricky and personally profitable deal and was celebrating with the investment group. There were about ten of us having dinner and drinking champagne. This couple came into the restaurant, and one of the people at the table knew them. He called them over and introduced me to Rose and

Stanley Clarkson. They were in their early sixties and from Florida. He was semiretired and had made his money in commercial real estate. They were enjoying an extended stay in London that had started as a fortieth-anniversary vacation trip.

"They joined us and I found myself becoming friends with them, at first just casually getting together for the occasional dinner. They had sublet an apartment, and our relationship eventually evolved into a personal one with my being their houseguest whenever I was in London. They grew to be almost like surrogate parents for me. They provided a comfortable atmosphere where I could relax and just be me…something I had not been able to do for a long time."

He paused as a moment of sadness swept over him. A lump formed in his throat. He knew talking about it was going to be difficult, but he hadn't realized just how much until the words started coming out of his mouth. He brushed a gentle kiss against her cheek. She reached up and clasped his hand, holding it against her chest. A subtle warmth filtered through his consciousness. He forged ahead with what he wanted to tell her—what he felt he *needed* to tell her.

"I've always made it a point to do business only with people who I knew could afford the financial risk. When you're dealing in highly speculative investments there's always a chance that something can go wrong. I've also made it a point not to do business with friends except for a few rare instances when I knew the people involved were able to separate personal and business.

"I really didn't know what the Clarksons' financial situation was, other than the outer trappings of maintaining an apartment in London in addition to a home in Florida. Stanley had mentioned on several occasions that he had some money set aside that he would be willing to invest if I had something I thought would be good. Then, almost by accident, I had a deal dumped in my lap that seemed like it would be perfect for them.

"I talked to Stanley and Rose about it, making sure they both thoroughly understood the risks involved. I had known the Clarksons for about six months by then, and we had become very close, much more so than I had thought possible. But when they handed me that check an ominous feeling came over me, almost like a voice telling me not to take it. I nearly backed out of the deal at the last minute."

A little sigh of resignation escaped his throat before he could stop it. "I wish I'd listened to that voice, because a few weeks later the deal fell apart. It wasn't anyone's fault. Everything was aboveboard and honest. It was just one of those things that happen in the world of high-risk business ventures, and everyone accepts the possibility. But this time it was different. This time I had become personally involved with one of the investors."

Dylan shifted his weight, more in an effort to try to shake loose the tension that had started to build inside him. It didn't help. He nudged Jessica forward onto her feet then stood up. He clasped her hand in his and they started walking again. He needed some sort of physical activity to ward off the pent-up tension.

She looked at him questioningly. "Are you okay?" She squeezed his hand. "I can feel the tension running through you."

He returned the squeeze. "Yeah, I'm fine. It's just

that I've never told anyone about this before and...well, I'm finding it a little difficult to talk about it.'' A soft feeling of closeness enveloped him when she rested her head against his shoulder as they walked along the trail.

He continued telling her about the Clarksons, wanting to get it all out before it overwhelmed him. ''By keeping a personal distance from those I was doing business with I had been able to develop an immunity to the emotional repercussions of a business deal that went sour. On those few occasions when it happened, I would simply tell the investors that the deal had fallen through and explain as best I could exactly why and what had happened, then I would move on. It was all cut-and-dried.

''But nothing had prepared me for the reality of having to tell Stanley and Rose that their money was gone. My gut twisted into a thousand knots, and I literally felt sick to my stomach when I gave them the bad news. The only saving grace to the situation was that they could afford the loss...'' His words trailed off as a hard lump settled in the pit of his stomach. ''At least that's what I thought.''

Dylan glanced up at the sky, noting the gathering storm clouds that were beginning to block out the sun. A cool breeze rustled through the trees sending a shiver across his skin. ''They were understanding, but it didn't take long for me to realize that the monetary loss was very significant for them. Just that knowledge upset me, but then something happened that hit me like nothing else in my life ever had and left me totally devastated.''

He swallowed, not at all happy with the confusing mixture of emotions that churned inside him. ''Stanley put his arm around Rose's shoulder and said that as long as they had each other their love would pull them through any crisis. His words, attitude and gracious manner in the face of adversity had produced an overwhelming guilt and remorse in me unlike anything I had ever experienced before, even though my dealings had all been ethical and straightforward. It was a moment that touched me on the deepest level of despair. That happened three months ago, and it's preyed on my conscience ever since that day.''

Jessica stopped walking, which brought Dylan to a halt. Her eyes showed a deep concern that carried over into her voice. "Is that how and why you ended up here?"

It was a valid question, as much as the one that had continued to circulate through his mind from that day—the question that asked what it must be like to be able to share that much love and devotion with someone special. He placed a gentle kiss on her lips. Would he ever be privileged to have that kind of love and devotion in his life? Could Jessica be that person? Or would it be something elusive that would always be just beyond his reach?

"Yes, that's how and why I came to be in the cabin. I managed to salvage their money from the collapsed deal, but it didn't do anything to stop my mounting guilt. Even now, three months later, it still haunts me. It's what made me realize that I needed to make some drastic changes in my life and that I needed a place of quiet and solitude to work them out.''

Dylan had almost told her about how he had recouped the Clarksons' money...the whole story...but had decided against it at the last moment. It had been difficult, but he had finally managed to get back part of their investment from the collapsed deal. He had made up the difference out of his own pocket without telling the Clarksons that the money had come from him personally. He knew them well enough to know that they would not have accepted the money if they had known it was his. It was a small gesture, one that had no real financial impact on his bank account, but something he felt he had to do. It was not enough, but he hadn't known what else to do other than again offer his sincerest apologies.

A wave of sadness swept over Jessica, almost as if she were able to personally touch the disheartened state he had described. Her words were soft and emotion laden. "I'm sorry."

"Oh?" He brought her hand to his lips and kissed her palm. A hint of a grin pulled at the corners of his mouth in sharp contrast to the heartfelt words he had used to explain his concerns. "And just what is it that you're sorry for?"

She paused for a moment, trying to find the proper words. She refused to be deterred by his apparent attempt to lighten the mood. "I'm sorry I gave you such a bad time about why you wanted to use the cabin. I had no business trying to pry into your personal situation by insisting on answers that you were obviously not willing to give. I should have respected your privacy and backed off, rather than intruding into your need for solitude. As you said, Justin did promise you the use of the cabin, and I was supposed to be in New York."

His features softened as most of the tension left his face. She reached up and gently smoothed out the remaining worry wrinkle that furrowed his forehead, then offered a hesitant smile.

"Is there anything I can do? Something that will help ease the situation for you?"

He put his arm around her shoulder. "You've already helped a great deal. You allowed me someone to tell about what happened. I feel better now that I've been able to get the words out. It's like a huge weight has been lifted from my shoulders. This has been churning inside me for months. It's put my entire life into a tailspin. I didn't know what to do or which way to turn. It's really been eating me up inside."

Just being able to verbalize his inner turmoil had been a great relief. He pulled her into his embrace and placed a tender kiss on her lips, one that spoke of caring yet conveyed a sensuality that defined the passion that embodied Dylan Russell.

"As for your intruding…I'm very grateful that you did." His voice was a whisper, his words truly heartfelt. "Thank you…thank you for listening to me, for being here."

For the first time in his life Dylan was beginning to feel truly settled in his feelings and mind about a direction for his life. Had he finally been able to come to terms with the misplaced guilt that had been bothering him for the past three months? For the first time he believed that he could actually get on with his life…a life that would be far more productive than it had been in the past. And Jessica had played a major role in making it possible. Without having realized it at the time, he now knew that she had been an inspiration…a reason to set some goals for his life, to try for better things.

A shiver of panic brought his thoughts around to the here and now. His growing involvement with Jessica had been pushing at him, telling him that it had already gone beyond what he had been prepared to handle. She was everything a man could want—certainly everything he had ever wanted—but he wasn't sure quite how to define what was happening or what to do about it.

He lowered his head to hers and captured her mouth in a heated kiss, partly to drive away his doubts and fears and partly because he didn't seem to be able to keep his hands off her. Her arms circled his neck in response to his fervor. His kiss deepened as he pulled her body tighter against his. His tongue invaded the dark recesses of her mouth…teasing, exploring, tasting.

The wind picked up and the sky darkened as it filled with storm clouds. The scent of approaching rain filled the air. Dylan broke the kiss and glanced up at the sky. He brushed a soft kiss against her lips. "I think we'd better get back to the cabin before we get caught out here without an umbrella."

She glanced up at the stormy sky. "You're right."

He continued to hold her in his embrace and her arms remained around his neck. Neither of them made any effort to break the spell holding them together. He looked into her eyes. His breath caught in his throat, and the panic welled inside him. He had spent most of his adult life avoiding any situation with a woman that could end up requiring a commitment from him. But he had not been able to escape the tantalizing presence of Jessica McGuire. How easy it would be for him to be pulled into the depths of those eyes.

He nestled her head against his shoulder as he continued to hold her. She felt so good in his arms, as if she belonged there. He didn't want to let her go. The possibilities frightened him, but the reality wouldn't allow him to leave. Even with the bridge opened and the way clear, he had chosen to stay. He wanted to stay with Jessica.

A fine mist tickled lightly across their faces, but neither of them made any effort to start back to the cabin. The mist turned to drizzle then quickly became a shower, forcing them to abandon the embrace that had held them in a shared time of intimate warmth and caring.

He took her hand and set a fast pace along the trail back toward the cabin. His intention was serious, but his manner was light and fun filled. "Come on…we're going to be soaked to the skin if we don't hurry."

She laughed, enjoying the spontaneous moment. "We're too far from the cabin to even hope to get back there in time."

He came to an abrupt halt and pulled her into his arms, a teasing grin playing across his lips. "Then it won't do any harm if we stop long enough for me to do this." He captured her mouth with a sensual kiss that spoke volumes about his passion.

Eight

Jessica and Dylan burst through the door of the cabin bringing a rush of wind and water in with them. They had run nearly a mile through what had become a steady rain, pausing on the porch only long enough to remove their muddy boots and shake the water from their jackets.

"Soaked is right!" She hung her wet jacket on the coat hook, then went straight to the bathroom and grabbed a couple of towels. She tossed one to Dylan and used the other to towel dry her hair.

"I can't believe how quickly it went from sunny sky to rain." He wiped the water from his face and ruffled the excess water from his hair. "Is that normal for here?"

"Yes, it can be. When there's a series of storms coming in off the ocean, they can turn the weather around pretty quickly." A shiver darted through her body, a combination of her wet clothes and the cool air inside the cabin. "We need to get some heat in here to take the chill out of the air, then I'm going to climb into a hot, steamy shower until I'm thoroughly thawed out."

He pulled her into his arms and nibbled playfully at her earlobe. "That hot, steamy part sure sounds good." He dropped his voice to a low, seductive whisper. "Mind if I join you?"

She closed her eyes and allowed the warmth of his touch to flow over her, cutting into the chill. "Hmm...that sounds like a very practical idea." A sexy grin played around the corners of her mouth. "And we'll be conserving hot water, too."

Every time they came in physical contact, her reason and self-control seemed to vanish in a puff of smoke. She had never experienced anything like Dylan Russell and she still wasn't sure exactly how to handle the way he made her feel. The excitement tingling inside her remained cloaked in caution. She had never felt about anyone the way she felt about him, but a nagging uncertainty continued to tug at her senses. Each passing minute went toward confirming the love she felt, but the nagging caution told her she didn't have a clue about his true feelings. He said and did all the right things, but she had no idea what was going on inside him.

"I'll start a fire—" he gave her a quick wink "—then join you in the shower." He brushed a tantalizing kiss across her lips, then released her from his embrace.

She watched for a moment as he crumpled a newspaper in the fireplace, placed the kindling on top of it, added a couple of logs and struck a match. A tremor

of sweet anticipation rippled through her body. She
turned her attention to the shower and the unspoken
promise of another night of unbridled passion.

She dropped her wet clothes to the floor and stepped
into the inviting spray. The water cascaded over her
body. The steam rose around her creating a sensual
cocoon. A few minutes later the shower curtain parted
and Dylan joined her in the steamy swirl.

He stood behind her, wrapping his arms around her
body. He kissed the side of her neck, then across the
top of her shoulder. His hands skimmed down her rib
cage, along her hips and across her stomach before
finally cupping the underside of her breasts. The feel
of her wet skin added to his already stimulated con-
dition. Every glimpse of bare skin, every seductive
touch, the rise and fall of her breasts with each breath
she took…no woman had ever attacked his senses the
way she did. Just being in the same room with her
filled him with a longing unlike anything he had ever
experienced.

Things he had thought could never be a part of his
life suddenly seemed possible. Was it too much to
hope for? He slid one hand from her breast down her
stomach to her inner thigh. The heat of her excitement
radiated to his fingers as he stroked her womanhood.
She trembled, a physical sensation that ran through her
body and resonated to his as it invaded the feeble hold
he had on his control. Her soft moan reached his ears,
an earthy sound that stimulated his already heightened
senses. He inserted a finger between her feminine
folds, stroking the core of her being.

She gasped, then drew in a sharp breath as she
leaned back against his body. His arousal pressed
against her lower back. A throbbing intensity churned

deep inside her. She stretched her arms back until she was able to run her hands along the outer edge of his muscular thighs. Her legs trembled as she fought to keep them from buckling under her. His magic touch evoked the deepest emotions and most intense sensations. She jerked her head back and allowed the shower spray to wash over her face and run down her body.

Her entire being quivered until the convulsions consumed her and her legs gave out. Dylan caught her and cradled her to him. The steam swirled around them while the spray splashed down, enveloping their bodies in a sensual cloud. He placed a tender kiss on her lips then held her tightly in his arms as the water cascaded over them.

He stroked his fingertips across the smooth skin of her bottom while dipping his head to tease her hardened nipple with his tongue. He drew it into his mouth and suckled. It was a couple of minutes before he found enough of his voice to be able to speak without gasping for air.

He tucked her head against his shoulder, her wet hair clinging to her cheek. He smoothed it away. "Do you think we've been here long enough to have chased off the chill?"

"I don't know about you, but I'm certainly warm enough." She placed a soft kiss on his chest. She reached for his hardened manhood, sending a tingle running up her arm. Her voice took on a husky quality. "Besides, if we don't get out of here soon there won't be any hot water left."

He turned off the water, then gently moved her hand away from his arousal. His voice was half teasing and half serious. "If you don't stop that I won't be able to get out of this bathtub for a while."

They stepped out of the tub. He grabbed a couple of large towels, wrapping one of them around her. He placed a loving kiss on her lips before drying himself off. They each dressed quickly, Jessica choosing a warm robe and Dylan pulling on some sweatpants and a sweatshirt, then they settled in front of the fireplace. The heat radiated into the room, infusing them with warmth and wrapping them in the softness of shared emotions.

It had been an eye-opening twenty-four hours for Jessica. She had made love with the most exciting man she had ever known and had admitted to herself that she had fallen in love with him in spite of the fact that she hadn't wanted to. But the most surprising of all was the real person she had discovered behind the playboy persona he presented to the world. Her thoughts turned to what he had told her about Rose and Stanley Clarkson. She had felt the tension running through his body as he told her about what had happened. It was blatantly apparent how difficult it had been for him to talk about it and even more so about how deeply it had affected him.

A warm feeling settled over her. He had chosen to share that very personal part of his life with her, something he had never told to anyone else. She had never felt more close to anyone than she had to him at that moment, a closeness that came from a deep emotional level totally separate from the physical desires that jumped into high gear whenever he looked at her.

It had filled in the missing pieces to the preconceived concept she had carried of him. It had given her insight into the whole man, not just the image. She had a clear picture in her mind of what she wanted, and that picture was a portrait of Dylan. She snuggled into his arms and rested her head against his shoulder. She felt safe, protected and cared for. It was a feeling she didn't ever want to lose. A little tremor reminded her that all was not perfect. Maybe she knew what she wanted, but she didn't have any idea if he had made any provisions for her as part of his future.

Dylan held her cradled in his arms. He kissed her forehead and her cheek. "You're very quiet."

"I was enjoying the fire, the warmth—" she looked up into his eyes "—and just being here with you."

"Me, too." He wasn't sure how to respond to her statement. He had never felt so comfortable with another person. He wanted her to be a part of his life, a part of his future. He didn't want to lose her. But he didn't know what to do. The magnitude of everything that had happened to him, everything that had gone on inside him, during the past few days, had nearly overwhelmed him. But the one thing that scared him the most was the idea of a commitment to a relationship. He had been that route before and it had been a disaster.

His fears pulled him in one direction while his desires tore him in another. And in the middle of this tug-of-war existed confusion far beyond anything he thought possible. A shiver of apprehension darted up his spine. He held her tighter. If only he could figure out the right thing to do.

The gentle patter on the roof said that the rain had tapered off to a light shower. They had dinner, then continued to bask in the glow of the fireplace as daylight faded away to be replaced by night.

"Jessica…" He trailed his fingers through the silky strands of her hair.

"Hmm?" She looked questioningly at him.

Dylan pulled her body hard against his. He wanted to tell her how much he cared about her, but the words stuck in his throat. He ran his hands inside her robe and across her bare back. He pulled her over on top of him. Instead of talking, he captured her mouth with an intense kiss, the heated passion exploding the moment their lips touched.

Her tantalizing taste filled his mouth and infused him with a need for much more. The kiss deepened. His tongue brushed hers. His ragged breathing matched hers in every respect. His fingers tickled across the silky fabric of her panties, then he slipped his hand inside the elastic band and stroked the curve of her bottom. It was so much more than sex, so much more than merely the physical. The magnitude of just how much more continued to frighten him.

Jessica's breathing became more labored with each passing moment. She ran her fingers through his hair while reveling in the sensations of his kiss and the tingling excitement of his hands caressing her body. Her heightened senses responded to each and every touch, no matter how light or brief. He pulled her robe open and slipped it off her shoulders.

He rolled over taking her with him until his body covered hers. He smothered her face with a flurry of kisses. His lips found the tautly drawn bud of her nipple. His excitement grew as he took it into his mouth. His hardened sex pushed against the fabric of his sweatpants.

Dylan tried to sit up as he gulped in a lungful of oxygen in an attempt to bring some control to his arduous pursuit. He drank in her beauty. The fire of passion glowed in the depths of her eyes. He devoured the enticing sight of her kiss-swollen lips. The flickering light from the fireplace enhanced the curve of her perfectly formed breasts as they rose and fell with her ragged breathing. The pounding in his chest sent the blood racing hot and fast through his veins, the rush resonating in his ears.

He yanked off his sweatshirt and tossed it on a chair. He took a deep breath as he rose to his feet, but it did nothing to calm his raging passions. With nearly frantic motions he managed to rid himself of the sweatpants. His legs quivered as the intense sensations swept through his body.

Jessica stared up at Dylan. The hard planes of his taut body glistened in the soft firelight. He was the most perfect specimen of male physique she had ever seen. Her pulse raced almost out of control. Everything about him shot her heartbeat into high gear. She had never been so brazen with any other man. The sexy glint in his eyes promised untold pleasures. She had also never made love on floor pillows in front of a fireplace in a mountain cabin. It was all so decadent, so uninhibited…and so very thrilling. She arched her hips and started to remove her panties.

"Let me do that."

His thick words and husky voice confirmed his obvious physical arousal. He sank to his knees, then snuggled his body between her legs. He trailed the tip of his tongue from the notch at the base of her throat to the valley between her breasts, sending a tremor of delight across the surface of her skin.

A quiver of anticipation rippled through her body. There wasn't any more guessing about what it would be like to make love to Dylan Russell. She knew…beyond a shadow of a doubt…that no one was more exciting or satisfied her needs and desires more completely.

He teased each nipple, then kissed the underside of each breast before continuing to trail the tip of his tongue down her stomach to the elastic band of her bikini panties. He nipped at the band with his lips, then secured it between his teeth and inched the panties down. A moment later his warm breath tickled through the downy softness covering her womanhood, sending a heated rush of desire coursing through her veins.

His most intimate of kisses exploded inside her causing her to cry out. She couldn't think straight. Reason and logic evaporated in an incendiary gust. Her entire body pulsed with excitement. He was everything she wanted…the only thing she wanted.

Dylan slipped her panties down her legs and tossed them aside, then quickly moved to cover her body with his. His frantic, almost-out-of-control desire for her swept aside more prudent thoughts of taking precautions. His rigid sex penetrated her feminine folds, filling her with the entire length of his arousal. The breath caught in his lungs. He paused a moment, savoring the exquisite sensations as her heat tightly encased his need.

He smothered her face in a frenzy of kisses. His hips rose and fell with the strong rhythm of his strokes. His ardor increased when she wrapped her legs around him, meeting each of his downstrokes with an upward thrust of her hips.

The layers of ecstasy built inside Jessica, filling her with a euphoria that surpassed anything she had ever known. They moved in rhythmic harmony, so in sync with each other's needs that it was as if they had been lovers for years. She sought out his mouth, the passion of his kisses. The texture of his tongue scraped against hers sending her last vestige of control out the window.

The convulsions crashed through her body with a heightened level of intensity. She clung tightly to Dylan as she threw back her head and gasped for air. The delicious sensations continued to course through her, reaching every part of her being.

She tried to speak, but could only manage one raspy word. "Dylan—"

He recaptured her mouth, cutting off any further attempts to say something. Every nerve ending in his body tingled with an intoxicating rapture. He gave one last deep thrust as he held her tightly in his arms. An earthy growl of pure, unbridled ecstasy clawed its way out of his throat as the hard spasms shuddered through his body. He quickly buried his face in her hair to prevent the words he was very close to saying…the words that revealed his deepest emotions and exposed every last shred of vulnerability he still tried to protect.

They remained on the pillows in front of the fire, arms and legs entwined, each clinging to the other. Neither wanted to let go, to break the physical connection between them. And the escalating emotional connection pulled them even closer together.

Dylan tucked a loose tendril of hair behind her ear, smoothed her hair back off her forehead, kissed her cheek, then brushed a soft kiss across her lips. He folded his arms around her again, nestling her head against his shoulder.

For three days they had been at the cabin together,

and in that time she had turned his life upside down and inside out. She had given his life purpose and been the impetus for the plan he had finally worked out for what to do with his future. He felt as if he'd known her forever and had never felt closer to anyone else.

He allowed the word *love* to drift through his mind, at first hesitantly then with greater resolve. But making a verbal commitment to a relationship…that still scared him. He knew he wanted to be with Jessica, that he wanted her to be part of his life. There was so much he wanted to say, but he didn't know exactly what to say or how to say it. Regardless of how strong his feelings for her were, making a permanent commitment to a lifelong relationship produced a high level of anxiety for him.

So he said nothing. He held her in his arms, stroked her skin, placed the occasional tender kiss on her cheek or forehead…and said nothing. He thought about love and about Jessica and how it all fit together. His thoughts were interrupted when she shifted her weight and snuggled farther in his arms.

The fire began to die out. She shivered as the chill settled over them. Dylan looked around at the clothes strewn across the floor, but there wasn't anything within reach to pull over them for warmth. As much as he disliked the notion of disturbing her, he knew he needed to get up. He gently nudged her.

"Are you awake?"

"Mmm…" She stretched and opened her eyes. "I think so."

"The fire is almost out. Either I need to put another log on the fire or—" he ran his fingers across the swell of her breasts, then sensually stroked her inner thigh "—we can do something else to create a little heat."

She grinned at him, her voice teasing. "Didn't we already create enough heat in this room?"

He returned her teasing and shot her a decidedly lustful look. "That was then—" he ran his hand across the curve of her hip, then cupped her bottom "—and this is now."

Her spontaneous laughter filled the air. "My, my, my. You seem to have an insatiable appetite this evening."

"Maybe we should do something about it." He captured her mouth with a renewed ardor that spoke of both desire and caring. He managed to maneuver her body without breaking the kiss until he was able to stand up while lifting her in his arms.

He carried her upstairs and deposited her gently in the middle of her bed. He stretched out next to her, reveling in the feel of her bare skin against his. She was right, his appetite was insatiable...at least where she was concerned. He couldn't get enough of her, both body and soul. Even if they never made love again, he would still want to be with her just to hear her voice and the sound of her laugh, to see the sparkle in her eyes.

He framed her face with his hands, not at all pleased with the slight tremble that he didn't seem able to control. He took a moment to simply drink in her beauty while wondering just how deeply he had gotten himself involved. Did the word *love* truly apply? He didn't have an easy answer, at least not one he was ready to accept.

His fingers trembled against her face, his touch sending a new wave of excitement coursing through her body. In the past twenty-four hours they had made love more times than she had since her divorce seven

years ago. And each time he had touched her on a
deeper level, reaffirming those feelings of love. And
now they were going to make love again.

Had she become as insatiable as she had teasingly
accused him of being? This was not like her. It flew
in the face of the logical and orderly life she had
worked so hard to develop, yet it all felt so very right.
She was caught up in a whirlwind of totally unexpected love with the most unlikely person she could
imagine. But that didn't make it any less real or true.
It was the type of spontaneous devil-may-care happiness she had never believed could be part of her life.

His mouth closed over hers, banishing everything
from her consciousness other than the ecstasy she
knew they would share.

Dylan stared up at the ceiling through the early-
morning light. He glanced at Jessica asleep in his
arms, seemingly without a care in the world. His heart
swelled with the euphoria that filled him just thinking
about her. But his joy remained tempered with caution.
He had been awake for probably an hour, his mind
racing with a myriad of conflicting thoughts. And at
the top of the list was his difficulty in separating lust
and love. The lust he knew well, but the unexpected
feelings of love that he had not been prepared for had
him confused.

Waves of uncertainty washed through him. He was
not sure how to handle the feelings. In fact, he had
never been so unsure of anything in his life. Should
he say something to her? Did he dare tell her how he
felt? She had opened up a world of possibilities for
him and had been responsible for him being able to

make some serious determinations about his future…a future he knew had to include Jessica McGuire.

He brushed a light kiss against her forehead, but continued to lie quietly so he wouldn't wake her. The enormity of what had been happening to him over the past three days nearly overwhelmed him. He had a plan for the future, a plan of what to do with his life and how to give back to the community. That was business. However, a plan for his personal life was not yet within his reach. It gleamed on the horizon, beckoning him forward. Was it real or only a mirage conjured up from his most deeply hidden dreams and desires?

Jessica stirred, immediately drawing his attention away from the bothersome thoughts and focusing on the enticing woman cradled in his arms. He watched her, not knowing whether she was still sleeping or awake. After a few minutes he closed his eyes in hopes of going back to sleep, but he couldn't turn off his thoughts.

Dylan wasn't the only one trying to sort out uneasy thoughts. She'd been awake for several minutes trying to get a clear picture in her mind of how things stood…of what the future held. Was it a future that included Dylan as part of her life? With all her heart she hoped so. She loved him, that she knew for sure. But what were his feelings toward her? She knew he cared about her very much, but did he love her? Could he possibly love her as much as she loved him?

It wasn't the only thing troubling her in the early-morning hours. The spontaneity that exploded between them in front of the fireplace had led to their making love without taking any precautions. That same heated passion carried over to the second time they had made love after he had carried her upstairs. It was a terrible lapse of good sense that had started preying on her mind even as she snuggled in his arms before she fell asleep. Had the same worry occurred to Dylan as well?

It only took one careless moment, and the entire course of her future could be drastically altered. The possibility of an unplanned pregnancy by a man who might not even want a child had given her a troubled night. She tried to clear her mind of the worrisome possibility. What was done couldn't be changed. She now had more immediate concerns that must be handled as soon as possible. She needed to have a serious discussion with Dylan, one that didn't include any touching. Her thinking needed to be clear and on track, not muddled by the desires he stirred in her. She had to know what to expect from him, what their future together would be...or if they even had a future together.

She slowly opened her eyes and stretched. She caught a quick glimpse of the worried expression on his face before he realized she was watching him. He quickly replaced it with a smile.

"Good morning." He kissed her on the forehead while smoothing her hair away from her face.

"Good morning to you, too." She tried to project an upbeat manner. She reached out and lightly touched his cheek, feeling the overnight growth of whisker stubble. Nothing would make her happier than to wake up every day with his arms wrapped around her. If only she knew what the future held.

They remained in the warmth of the bed for a while, each content to not speak and enjoy the comfortable moments of the morning—the sun filtering in through the window and the birds providing a cacophony of sounds. Then Jessica sat up, her brow furrowed slightly as she stared toward the window.

She glanced at Dylan. "Do you hear that? It sounds like trucks and voices."

She slipped out of bed, looking around the room for her clothes. Then she smiled. "Oh...I forgot. We left our clothes scattered around the living room."

He returned her smile as he sat up, swinging his long legs over the side of the bed. He grasped her hand, tugged her toward him, then wrapped his arms around her hips. His warm breath tickled her bare skin as he placed a soft kiss between her breasts. A little shiver of delight rippled through her body. Then the sound caught her attention again.

"There...did you hear that?"

"Yes." Dylan released her from his embrace and climbed out of bed. A hint of concern clouded his features as he peeked through the miniblinds. "I don't see anything, but we'd better get some clothes on just in case."

Nine

Jessica stood on the porch with Dylan and watched as the power company truck continued on down the road. The bridge was open and now electricity had finally been restored to the area. A sadness settled over her, seeping into every corner of her reality. She knew their idyll had reached the end. The time had come to leave the fantasy world that had totally captivated her senses and return to the real world of responsibility and commitment.

A level of anxiety welled up inside her, nothing too uncomfortable, yet a distinct feeling all the same. The last two days of their time together had been perfect— long walks in the woods, cozy evenings in front of the fireplace and nights filled with a passion unlike any she had ever known.

As she turned to go back inside the cabin, he slipped his arm around her. A shiver of trepidation darted up her spine. She reached up and laced her fingers with his where his hand rested on her shoulder. The warmth of his touch brought a calm to her internal jitters. She closed her eyes and took a deep breath. She loved him and didn't want to lose him, but her practical side said a relationship needed a commitment and two people who both wanted it to work. She had to know where he stood and what he wanted.

A heaviness pressed on her shoulders, a moment of sorrow she feared would soon be all she had left of what she hoped would be a love to last a lifetime. She tried to still the growing uneasiness that had rapidly overshadowed her joy. She also needed to pack her suitcase so she could return to Seattle and her job. She eased her hand out of his grasp. The moment she broke the physical contact with him, she felt as if she had lost a little piece of her life. It was too late to turn back. She lived in the real world, she couldn't do any less. She headed for the stairs. "I have some things to do."

"Anything I can help you with?"

"I won't be long." She paused at the bottom of the stairs. Her anxiety level shot up. She didn't dare look at him if she wanted to maintain her determination. "When I finish I think we need to talk."

"Uh...sure. What is it you want to talk about?"

She heard the surprise in his voice. Could he be oblivious to their need to discuss the future? Had she misjudged him that badly? No, it was just her anxieties showing. She had discovered a caring and compassionate man...someone who had been so devastated by what happened to the Clarksons that it had sent his entire life into chaos, someone who wanted to give back to the community and help others.

"I think we need to talk about the future." She hurried upstairs before he had a chance to respond.

A little tremor of apprehension made its way through Dylan's body as he watched her disappear up the stairs. The future…it was something that had been on his mind all morning. He didn't want to lose her from his life. He could not take a chance on things somehow working out by themselves. He needed to tell her how he felt and what he had been thinking about ever since they got out of bed a couple of hours ago.

He glanced toward the stairs, then left the cabin and went to the garage where he had parked his car. He grabbed his cell phone and the charger. Now that power had been restored he could charge the drained battery, then he could start making reservations. The more he thought about what he wanted to do the more excited he became at the prospect.

He plugged in the phone charger in the kitchen, then went upstairs in search of Jessica. He couldn't stop the grin that pulled at the corners of his mouth. Yes, they needed to talk about the future…a future that excited him more and more with each passing minute.

The sight stopped him at the bedroom door. "Jessica?" He crossed the room, took hold of her shoulders and turned her around to face him. An uncomfortable wariness churned inside him. He searched her face for some sort of explanation, something that would tell him everything was okay…that his sudden uneasiness was unfounded. Her face held no reassurances to ease his mind.

"You're packing?" He couldn't keep the anxiety out of his voice. "Are you going somewhere? I thought you wanted to talk."

She tried to swallow her apprehension, but it stuck in her throat. She returned to her packing, placing the last item in her suitcase and closing the lid. She continued to stare at the suitcase, afraid to turn around and face him. He seemed so genuinely shocked and confused.

"Jessica…answer me…please." A hesitation and uncertainty crept into his words. "Are you…are you going somewhere?"

She drew in a steadying breath in an attempt to still the hard tremors of distress that throbbed inside her. She loved him, but that wasn't enough. It took two people committed to a relationship to make a success of it. She had no idea how he felt or what he wanted. And if their lapse in taking precautions the last time they made love resulted in her being pregnant…

A shiver of apprehension darted through her body followed by a hard surge of fear. Either way she needed to know where things stood between them. It couldn't be put off until later when it would be far more awkward. She had to know now. She turned to face him.

"Uh, I've been giving a lot of thought to us…to the future—"

"Me, too." He cut off her words as he pulled her into his arms. His heart pounded with the uncertainty that tried to grab hold of him. He knew he had to say what was on his mind as quickly as possible.

"The time we've spent together has been very important to me. I came here to try to work things out, and I've gotten so much more than I had anticipated. I was able to formulate a plan for my financial seminars and at the same time found someone who is very special to me—" he brushed a loving kiss against her lips as much to calm the churning inside him as to taste her sweetness ''—someone I care about very much.'' He had come within a breath of saying he loved her, but a sudden rush of panic prevented him from getting the exact words out of his mouth.

''I came here confused and guilt ridden and not able to figure out how to deal with it, but now I feel regenerated, and it's all because of you. I'm ready to set out and face the world again. I know what I want out of life—'' he swallowed down the lump in his throat ''—and you're definitely part of it.''

He'd said it. He hadn't used the word *love*, but just being able to say how much he cared for her created an excitement in him that quickly escalated toward euphoria. He hugged her tightly against his body. The future was theirs. Everything was perfect. He wanted to do something very special for her, something to show her just how deep his feelings were and how much he cared. Even if he hadn't been able to get the proper words together, what better way to show her that he loved her than to give her the world.

''Come away with me, Jessica. I want to show you all the places you've never been.''

Her words were hesitant. ''I don't understand. You're saying we should take a vacation?''

He saw the confusion cloud her features, but he refused to allow his enthusiasm to be dampened by the caution that tried to grab hold of his reality. ''No, not a vacation…a whirlwind adventure from one romantic city to another. We'll travel Europe together. I want to give you palaces by day and the moon and stars by night. We'll spend long lazy hours in each other's arms and make love until dawn.''

She furrowed her brow as her confusion deepened. "You mean just get on an airplane and go?"

"Yes. We could leave as soon as you're ready." He looked at her expectantly. "What do you say?"

He touched his fingertips to the frown that spread across her forehead. A rising feeling of trepidation finally broke through his euphoria, telling him something was wrong. "What's the matter? You seem worried about something."

"I have a job to tend to, bills to pay. I can't possibly take off on a whirlwind vacation on the spur of the moment just because it would be fun. My life isn't structured that way."

A wave of relief swept through him accompanied by a soft chuckle. "Is *that* all." His sudden attack of anxiety had been groundless. Her concern was money. Money certainly wasn't a problem for him. All he needed to do was make sure she understood that it didn't stand in their way, then she'd see it wasn't a problem for her, either. A soft warmth settled inside him. Everything he wanted was right here. The future would be everything he had envisioned.

"Is that all?" A hard lump formed in her throat, and a sudden jolt of fear churned in her stomach. Had she heard him correctly? Was he saying that her commitment to her job wasn't important? How could he possibly assume she would be willing to just fly away with him as if she had no responsibilities? Had she been wrong in believing he had changed? Was he still the globe-trotting playboy who lived in a whirlwind world of excitement but knew nothing about commitment and responsibility? Her throat tightened so much that she couldn't even swallow. Surely there must be

a mistake. He couldn't have meant that the way it sounded.

"You don't need to worry about the money. I have more than enough for us. We could live comfortably for the rest of our lives without having any money worries. You can take a sabbatical from work without having any concerns about your bills."

Jessica recoiled in shock, wrenching loose from his embrace. She felt the sting just as if he had literally slapped her across the face. Her disappointment quickly turned to hurt and anger. Years of pent-up resentment over the unresolved issues of her life suddenly leaped in front of her, born anew. A sick churning grabbed hold of her.

It was her ex-husband all over again. How could she have been so foolish as to allow herself to be taken in a second time by the same type of handsome features and the same charming manner? It was *his* money, so her desire for a career didn't matter. Well, not again. Not this time.

"That was the same thing my ex-husband thought. He had the money, he paid the bills, so he called the shots, and my life and needs didn't matter." There was a bitterness in her voice, yet a hint of pain just beneath the surface. "Well, this isn't about money. It's about responsibility and commitment, two words that apparently aren't in your vocabulary. My ex didn't see it that way, and obviously neither do you. I've worked very hard to make a career for myself, one I'm very proud of, and I have a responsibility to my clients and have a commitment to them which I intend to honor." Her voice cracked as hurt regained the upper hand over her anger. "I'm sorry you consider that inconsequential."

A combination of confusion and anger came out in his words. "What the hell are you talking about?"

"I'm talking about responsibility for your choices and making a commitment to something—" she swallowed back a sob in a frantic attempt to maintain her composure "—making a commitment to a relationship. It's something my ex couldn't do, and I'm not going to allow myself to be caught in that trap again."

He spit out the angry words. "I'm not your ex-husband any more than you're my ex-fiancée. Stop trying to put me into that mold."

She blinked back the threat of tears as she turned away from him. A horrible sense of loss invaded her consciousness. She had done the one thing she didn't want to do. She had lost her heart to another charming scoundrel, and now she was paying the price. She would never give Dylan the satisfaction of seeing her cry, of knowing how much he had hurt her.

She picked up her suitcase. "I fell totally and completely under your spell and thought we had something special. But what you've offered me is a proposition, not a commitment."

She held her breath, hoping against hope he would tell her he loved her and offer the commitment she craved. She stood motionless for what seemed like an eternity. His silence spoke louder than any words. There wasn't much left to say. With a heavy heart she started toward the bedroom door.

"Justin offered you the use of the cabin, so you're welcome to stay on if you want. The time of a carefree getaway is over for me. I need to return to the *real* world, to accept my responsibilities and honor my commitments…something *I* take very seriously."

Dylan watched in stunned disbelief as she walked

out of the bedroom and started down the stairs. He remained riveted to the spot, unable to make his legs move. He felt as if a hot knife had been twisted in his gut. His mind drifted in and out of reality as he tried to comprehend what had happened between the moment of euphoria when he told her he cared for her very much and a few minutes later when she told him he didn't know anything about responsibility and commitment and went on to compare him to her ex-husband. Had he blacked out and somehow missed something that connected the two extremes? He searched his memory, desperate for a clue…anything that would make some sense of what happened.

He heard the front door close. Total and complete panic grabbed him. He raced downstairs and out of the cabin just as she closed her car trunk. He hurried across the porch and took hold of her arm before she could slide in behind the steering wheel.

"Don't leave. Stay with me…please."

She stared at the ground, refusing to make eye contact with him. "I can't…I have to go home…to get back to work."

"What's going on here, Jessica?" He took a calming breath, but it didn't help. "Talk to me." He certainly wasn't a stranger to life in the fast lane, but this was way too fast even for him. One minute they were arguing over some silly little thing, and a couple of days later she was the single most important person in his life. Everything seemed to be spinning out of control and it scared him. So many things he wanted to say to her, chief among them being how much he loved her, but the words refused to materialize.

Her voice was soft, barely above a whisper. "I don't know what else there is that I can say."

They stood in silence for several seconds while Jessica waited for him to reply. She desperately wanted him to say something, but again there was only silence. She swallowed several times, trying to force the sick churning back down her throat. She got in her car. A single tear slid down her cheek, followed by another and then another until they had turned into a steady flow.

She tried to convince herself that it was just one of those things, a few exciting days tucked away in a mountain cabin with an exciting and sexy man. She knew she would never get over him. There would always be an empty place in her heart where Dylan Russell had lived for those enchanted days and passionate nights. She glanced in the rearview mirror and caught one last glimpse of him before her car rounded the curve. The sight tore at what little composure she still possessed. He looked as devastated as she felt.

Dylan continued to stare down the road at the spot where her car had disappeared around the bend. He felt numb inside except for a hollow ache. His heart had gone with her, leaving a gaping hole in his life. And he didn't know how it happened or what to do about it. For years he had been running from the turmoil of an emotional commitment. Even the thought of becoming involved in a true relationship frightened him. But now he had found something that frightened him even more—the thought that he might have blown any chance of having Jessica as part of his life. And if he didn't do something quickly it would probably end up costing him Justin's friendship as well.

He hunched his shoulders against the cold shiver that swept through his body. He suddenly felt more alone than he ever had in his entire life. He returned to the cabin and plopped on the couch, too distraught to move or even think except for the one thought that penetrated the fog of his mind. He had to win Jessica back.

It seemed like hours before he was able to focus his thoughts and force himself to move. He went to his cell phone, checking the battery to make sure it had charged up enough to use.

Jessica hugged the stuffed bear to her body. It had been a gift from Dylan when she was sixteen years old and was the only one of her stuffed animal collection that she still owned. Even though it had a torn ear and a missing eye, she cherished it dearly. She propped the bear up on her fireplace mantel and stared at it.

"Well, Mr. Buttons, surely you must have an opinion about all of this." A sigh of despair escaped her throat as the emotion once again overwhelmed her. "I've never loved anyone as much as I love him, but I can't enter into a relationship without having a commitment equal to the one I'm willing to give. He wanted me to run away with him, but that's just what it would be—running away. It would have been a wonderful escape, but eventually I'd need to climb down off cloud nine and come back to earth. I can't ignore my responsibilities. That's just the way I am."

She ran her fingertips across the bear's face and straightened his vest. "Was I wrong? Did I push him too much? Should I just have accepted whatever he was willing to give and hope that maybe…someday…"

A sob caught in her throat, and tears welled up in her eyes again. She had cried all the way back to Seattle, so how could she possibly have any tears left? For someone who was normally so self-assured and decisive she had certainly made a muddled mess of everything.

An insistent pounding at her door jerked her back to reality. She quickly wiped the tears away with her hand, ran her fingers through her hair to fluff it up, then opened the door.

"Justin...this is a surprise." Something about his expression pushed at her anxiety level. She stepped aside so he could come in. "I've only been home for about three hours...just long enough to unpack and run a load of clothes through the washer and dryer."

He nervously shifted his weight from one foot to the other. "Are you alone?" His gaze darted around the room as if he was searching for something. "I'm not interrupting anything, am I?"

"No...of course not. When did you get back from your flight?"

Justin called over his shoulder as he headed for the kitchen. "I got home yesterday morning." He opened the refrigerator and grabbed a bottle of beer. "Can I get you anything while I'm here?"

"No, nothing for me." She joined her brother in the kitchen, watching him closely as he twisted the cap off the bottle. She knew him well enough to know there was something specific on his mind even though he hadn't said so.

"Uh, you'll never guess who I heard from a couple of weeks ago. You remember Dylan Russell, don't you?" He leaned casually against the doorjamb as if the question had no more significance than inquiring about the weather, but she could see the nervousness working through him.

She forced a laugh. "Of course I remember him. How could I forget when you talk about him all the time?" A quick flash of melancholy hit her. There was no way she would ever be able to forget Dylan. His reality was permanently imprinted on her life.

"Well, I got an e-mail from him a couple of weeks ago asking me if he could use our cabin for a week or so. It coincided with the time you said you were going to be in New York, so I sent him the key. Fortunately he must have changed his mind about using it." Justin laughed nervously. "It's a good thing because it probably wouldn't have been wise to have you and Dylan staying there at the same time."

"Well…that's not quite accurate." Now his sudden appearance at her door and his obvious nervousness made sense. He wanted to know if anything had happened between Dylan and her.

Justin looked questioningly at his sister. "Oh?"

"I was surprised to find someone there when I arrived and even more surprised when that someone turned out to be Dylan. He said you had given him the use of the cabin." She could tell from the expression on Justin's face that he expected her to say more. They normally confided in each other, but this was different. This was much too painful for her. She wasn't ready to talk about it yet. Maybe if she quickly shifted the conversation in another direction he would take the hint and let the subject drop.

"Are you home for a while now or are you scheduled out on another flight right away?" Jessica asked.

"Nothing for a week. I'll be around the office quite a bit, especially with the partnership in the works." He wandered into the living room and made himself comfortable.

She followed him, curling into the corner of the couch in a manner she hoped would appear casual in spite of the tension pulsing through her body. She looked up to find Justin staring at her. Her tension increased, accompanied by the unnerving way his gaze seemed to be saying he was concerned about her. She self-consciously ran her fingers through her hair.

She tried to make light of what had become a very serious moment. "What's the matter…do I have dirt on my face?"

"No, but your eyes are red as if you've been crying. Are you all right? You look like hell."

She forced a nervous laugh. "Thank you. That's just the kind of thing a girl wants to hear." She knew she had to tell him something to satisfy his obvious curiosity. "I'm tired, that's all. There was quite a storm on the Peninsula. The power was out when I arrived and was only restored this morning. The high water and debris washing downstream had the bridge closed for a couple of days, too. So…I really didn't get too much sleep. And I think I'm coming down with a cold. My eyes have been watering and itching."

"Oh, I see." He took a swallow from his bottle of beer. "I thought maybe Dylan's being there had caused you a problem. He's a lot of fun, and we've been good friends since our freshman year of college, but it wouldn't be advisable to take him too seriously. He goes through women like some people go through Kleenex. I know for a fact that he has no interest in settling down and staying in one place. Any woman who became involved with him would end up with a broken heart."

A spark of irritation exploded inside her. She tried to shove it down, to appear unconcerned. "You're the

last person who should be handing out advice about
dating and relationships. You and I both have one bad
marriage strike against us. And your track record with
women since your divorce certainly isn't anything to
brag about.''

Justin sat up straight, his gaze shifting nervously
around the room. ''We're not talking about my track
record, we're talking about Dylan's. He's one of my
best friends, and I probably know him better than anyone, but…''

Except me. Justin's words faded off into the back-
ground as her thoughts drifted to her conversations
with Dylan where he shared his secrets with her. She
knew about his being shafted by his fiancée on their
wedding day and about what had happened to Rose
and Stanley Clarkson…things Justin didn't know.

A new level of confusion pushed at her. Dylan had
shared deeply personal things with her. He had trusted
her with his pain and vulnerability. Didn't that say
something? Didn't that show how much he cared
about her? Her eyes misted over as another wave of
despair washed through her. If he could do that, then
why couldn't he tell her he loved her?

Her attention was drawn back to what Justin was
saying.

''…am only telling you this for your own good.''

She made no attempt to withhold her irritation. ''I
don't need you to run my life for me. I'm capable of
making my own decisions.''

''I didn't say you weren't.'' Justin carried his empty
beer bottle into the kitchen, followed closely by Jessica. ''It's just that you've never come up against anyone like Dylan before. He plays in the big leagues and
lives in the fast lane. He's left a trail of broken hearts

all over the world. I don't want you to end up as another one.''

''Apparently I need to remind you...*again*...that you're my brother, not my father. I'm thirty-one years old and have been married and divorced. I'm self-supporting and travel all over the country as part of my career. I'm not exactly some naive little teenager. I've been around. I don't need you selecting my friends for me...or my dates. I can make those decisions myself without any help from you.''

Justin whirled around and stared at her, his jaw set in a hard line. ''You may be thirty-one years old but...'' He fought the grin that tugged at the corners of his mouth.

She gave him a loving, sisterly punch in the shoulder. ''You'd better get out of my face or I'll call Aunt Phoebe and invite her to be your houseguest for a monthlong visit, and I'll tell her you insist that she bring cousin Lily with her.''

Justin took two quick steps back as he raised his hands in a gesture of surrender. ''Mea culpa...I give up!'' A soft chuckle escaped his throat. ''You're just ornery enough to do it, too.''

He put his arm around her shoulder and walked back into the living room with her. ''You're still my baby sister, Jess, and I reserve the right to worry about you.''

She gave him a loving hug. ''I know, and thank you for caring.''

''So, this puts us back to where we started. Are you okay?''

''I will be.'' A sigh turned into a sob as she drew in a steadying breath, then expelled it. ''But I'm afraid your advice is a little late. I haven't felt this way about any man since my divorce.''

Justin awkwardly shifted his weight from one foot to the other, his body language confirming his discomfort at the unexpected turn in the conversation. ''Uh, I'm not sure exactly what you mean.''

''I mean I'm very attracted to him. In fact—'' her voice dropped to a whisper as she stared at the floor ''—I think I just might be falling in love with him.'' It was the biggest understatement of all time.

''I hope you know what you're doing, Jess.''

She gave a halfhearted laugh, as much bittersweet as anything else. ''I can't imagine what I said that gave you that impression.''

He smiled encouragingly. ''Well, if things turn out badly for you I promise not to say 'I told you so.'''

''I don't think there's anything to worry about. I doubt I'll be seeing Dylan again.'' A sob caught in her throat, accompanied by the now-familiar sick churning in her stomach. ''Everything ended at the cabin.''

''I'm sorry, Jess. I wish there was something more appropriate I could say to make you feel better.'' He glanced toward the kitchen. ''Have you had any dinner?''

''I'm not very hungry.''

''Let's go out and get something to eat—my treat.''

The melancholy settled over her, making her realize how empty she felt inside—empty and numb. ''I don't think so, not tonight.'' She looked up at her brother, mustering as much of a smile as she could manage. ''Maybe some other time.''

''Do, uh, do you want to talk about it? I don't have any plans. I could stay with you tonight if you'd like.''

"Thanks, Justin, but it's not necessary. I'll be fine. I just need to sort out a few things in my mind."

A worried expression crossed his face. "Are you sure? I don't mind staying."

She forced an upbeat manner that she really didn't feel. "I'm sure...now go on."

"I'll call you in the morning. If you need anything, I'll be home."

She escorted her brother out the front door, then watched as he drove away. Once again she was alone with the emotional turmoil that churned inside her. Telling her brother that she might be falling in love with Dylan had been an out-and-out lie. She could tell from Justin's expression that he didn't really believe what she had told him but had the good sense not to say so. She had already fallen deeply in love with the charmer in spite of every reason she had given herself for not allowing it to happen.

And never very far from the forefront of her thoughts was the possibility that she could be pregnant. Maybe things would look better in the morning after a good night's sleep. A single tear rolled down her cheek. How was it possible for love to hurt so much?

The ringing phone broke the silence of the room. A surge of excitement raced through her body. Did she dare to hope that it would be Dylan? She took a deep breath to calm her nerves, then lifted the receiver.

"Hello." She waited a second, but no one replied. Then the line went dead. Her spirits sank to the depth of her consciousness. It was obviously a wrong number. She turned and went to the bedroom, her heart heavy with her despair.

* * *

Dylan replaced his cell phone in the charger cradle. The second he heard Jessica's voice the words froze in his throat and wouldn't come out. The hard knot in the pit of his stomach and his high level of anxiety told him how deeply he had become involved with her, how much he already missed her...and how much he loved her.

He had not been able to say those words, or any other words for that matter, to keep her from leaving. All he had been able to do was stand like a statue and watch her drive away. And just now, after spending several miserable hours alone in the cabin, he had phoned her with the same paralyzing results.

Had he totally driven her away with his inability to give her what she so obviously wanted and deserved? To make a commitment to her and to their relationship? Had she gone from his life for good? A sinking despair finally overcame him. He collapsed on the couch, leaned back and closed his eyes. Images of her face danced across the screen of his mind—her smile, the sparkle in her eyes, her delicious mouth.

The loss of either the woman he loved or his best friend was unacceptable, but the loss of both was unthinkable. Exposing all his fears and laying open his total vulnerability could not be any more painful than what he was going through right now, and certainly not as horrendous as a future that did not include Jessica. He drew in a deep breath and held it for several seconds before expelling it.

He had to do whatever it took to win her back and hopefully capture her love. But where to begin? He sat upright. He knew the answer to that...it had been with him all along, his very purpose in being at the cabin to begin with. In order to win her back he had to prove himself worthy of her trust. He needed to take the plan he had formulated for his financial seminars and put it into effect.

Dylan raced for the bedroom, taking the stairs two at a time. He grabbed a notebook and began making a To Do list. He would show Jessica he could offer her what she wanted.

Then he would ask her to share his life.

Ten

"Thanks, Glen." Dylan started toward the office door. "My attorney will contact your legal department. We'll be able to get started a month after the paperwork is signed. I have almost everything in place now…just a few more loose ends to tie up, then we're set."

"I want to thank you for bringing this project to me," Glen said. "I really like the way you've laid it out. Not only will this be something of benefit to the community, it meets the requirements for our public service programming as well. Let me know when you're ready, and I'll schedule the studio production time for you and we'll work out a broadcast schedule for our other stations in Los Angeles, Phoenix, Dallas, Chicago, Miami and New York."

The two men shook hands to seal their agreement, then Dylan left the television station manager's office.

It had been a busy week for him, and he had managed to accomplish everything on his list in record time. He had never worked so hard on anything in his life, nor had anything ever meant as much to him or been as important to his future—his and Jessica's.

Not an hour had gone by that he hadn't thought about her and yearned for the time he could present her with his accomplishments. Everything he had done had been with one purpose in mind...to erase the past and win her back.

He had offered to give her the world and had been crushed and confused when she'd turned him down. It had been a mistake on his part, one he did not intend to repeat. A shiver of apprehension invaded his thoughts and plans. He had tried several times to call her, but each time he had only gotten her answering machine. He had gone to her house three times, but no one had been home. He didn't know where she had gone.

Now that everything was set, he only had one thing left to do. He had to find her. He returned to his hotel room in downtown Seattle and dialed her phone number. And once again the machine answered.

He sat on the edge of the bed and surveyed his surroundings. Another hotel room. He had been in too many of them. He longed for the closeness of home and family that had never been part of his adult life; a real house instead of an apartment or another hotel room; and the woman he loved, to help him make it the kind of home he'd always wanted even though he had never admitted it until now. And more than just the woman he loved...also a family. His thoughts drifted to a place that he had always been afraid to go. Perhaps a son to carry on his name, someone to play ball with and take camping. Or maybe a daughter, a beautiful little girl who would look just like Jessica. A soft warmth settled over him. It was what he wanted most, and somehow he had to make it happen.

He dialed another number.

"Justin? It's Dylan." He didn't like the nervousness he heard in his own voice. "Where's Jessica? I've been trying for a week to find her. I've called several times and have even gone to her house."

"I'm, uh, not sure. Why are you looking for her?"

The edge of caution in Justin's voice caught Dylan off guard. He had heard it before, but never aimed in his direction. It raised a new level of anxiety within him.

"I need to talk to her. We have some things to work out." He tried to keep a tight rein on his emotions. He didn't want to get into a misunderstanding with Justin, but he had to find Jessica. "Some personal matters."

"Tell me, *good buddy*—" the antagonism in Justin's voice cut across the phone line, jumping Dylan's anxiety level up a notch "—what kind of *personal* business do you have with my sister?"

Dylan took a calming breath and put forth an extra effort to remain neutral in this conversation with Justin. "It's just that—*personal.*"

"Come on, Dylan, this is my sister we're talking about, not one of your many girlfriends *du jour*. I know how you are with women—"

"No, you don't!" Dylan's angry words cut Justin off in midsentence. "You know what you want to believe, or what you think is true. You seemed to get a kick out of believing that I had a different woman in my bed every night, so I never bothered to correct you, but that was your take on reality...not mine.''

He took a calming breath, unhappy with himself for getting angry at Justin. He tried to smooth it over. "I can understand your being concerned for her well-being, but this is private...just between Jessica and me. Now, do you know where she is?" The trepidation coursed through Dylan as he waited for Justin to say something. In a friendship that spanned seventeen years, this was the first time anger had ever flared between them.

After what seemed to Dylan like an eternity, Justin finally relented. "She's in New York. She was called back to finish that job that was postponed. She should be home tomorrow night.''

"Are you picking her up at the airport? I'll save you the trip.''

"No. I didn't know if I would be in town or not so she drove her car and left it in the long-term parking lot.''

"Tomorrow night?''

"Yep, her flight gets in about five o'clock.''

"Uh, Justin, while I've got you on the phone I'd like to talk to you about your purchase of the charter company.'' The mood quickly settled back into the type of relationship Dylan and Justin had always enjoyed.

Jessica kicked off her shoes and sank into the large overstuffed chair in her living room. She had been grateful for the activity of the New York project and the opportunity to concentrate her energy and efforts on something other than Dylan Russell, but it felt good to be home. She leaned back in the chair and closed her eyes, then the ringing doorbell brought her back to attention.

"Dylan!" When she opened the door, her heartbeat jumped into high gear and her mouth went dry. He was the last person she expected to see standing on her porch. He didn't say anything. He stood there staring at her with the oddest expression on his face, one she couldn't decipher. A strange combination of joy and hurt swept through her body, pulling apprehension along with it.

His steady, unrelenting gaze touched her nerves. She awkwardly shifted her weight, not sure what to say or do. Her pain shoved the joy aside. She quickly blinked away the misty film that started to form over her eyes. The only thing she was sure of was that she would rather die than shed another tear because of Dylan. A shiver darted across her nape, then down her spine. He just stood there, as if frozen to the spot. Why didn't he say something? The silence became deafening.

She forced herself to say, "What are you doing here?" She felt as if she were being torn in two: one part of her wanted him to fold her into his embrace and chase the pain away; the other part wanted to hide away from the nearly overwhelming desire coursing through her veins. It was all she could do to remain in place. An uneasiness welled up inside her. "Why are you looking at me like that?"

He reached out and lightly brushed his fingertips across her cheek. His voice cracked as he said, "I'm just comparing you to the mental image I've been carrying around ever since you drove away from me at the cabin."

She couldn't stop her hurt from lashing out at him.

"You mean when you stood there and didn't say a word after I gave you every opportunity to say something...anything that would have let me know if we had a future together?"

Her words sent a hard jolt of pain through him. He swallowed down his panic. He knew it wouldn't be easy. She had every reason to be hurt and angry. He saw the wariness in her eyes and read the attitude of her body language as she crossed her arms in front of her and took a step backward without inviting him to come inside.

"I mean when I was too scared of what I was feeling to say anything. In fact, I was too scared to even allow myself to think."

He took a steadying breath, then continued, "I wanted to do something special for you, to give you something that would show you how much I cared. I wanted to give you the world...literally."

"I didn't want the world."

"I know that now." She was so close, the physical contact too alluring. He couldn't resist the temptation any longer. He leaned his face into hers and brushed his lips softly against hers. He caressed her cheek with his fingertips, but stopped there.

"Oh, Jessica...you have no idea how much I've missed you. I'm sorry if I gave you the wrong impression. I didn't mean to detract from your job or make light of your career. I very much admire your independence and the way you've made a success of your life."

"Maybe we'd better go inside, rather than stand here in the open doorway." She stepped inside, and he entered the house behind her, closing the door after him. His words touched her deeply, especially after her ex-husband had done everything he could to discourage any independence on her part and had been adamantly against her having a career.

Dylan directed her over to the couch. Almost involuntarily, he reached inside his jacket pocket to make sure the small velvet box was still there...an action he had performed several times in the past hour. He took a deep breath, held it, then exhaled in an attempt to calm the nervous jitters racing through his body. He sat next to her.

"I want to tell you what I've been doing this past week. After you left the cabin I made several phone calls—"

"Phone calls? But there isn't a phone...." She furrowed her brow in confusion. "You mean you went down to the store to use the pay phone?"

"No, with the power restored I was able to get the cell phone from my car and recharge the battery. I set up several appointments for the next three days, then drove to Seattle and checked into a hotel. Since that time I've had meetings with various civic groups, the senior citizens council, the university's adult continuing-education department, one of the local television stations and an advertising agency.

"I've laid the groundwork for my financial seminars and have expanded the idea I had originally discussed with you. I've met with an attorney to set up a nonprofit foundation to run the clinics and maintain a Web site on the Internet. In addition to holding the live clinics, I'm also having them taped so they can air on television and the videos can be purchased by mail order and through the Web site."

He nervously cleared his throat. "I've also made arrangements to move to Seattle permanently."

Her insides shook so violently it took all her effort to keep it from showing. She wasn't sure where he was going with any of this, but the mere fact that he had sought her out to share his news was enough to make her heart swell with the love she felt for him. This man that she had at first assumed was just like her ex-husband had turned out to be nothing like him. Did she dare to hope that they had a chance for a life together?

Then the storm clouds of doubt again invaded her thoughts. He still had not offered her a commitment or even said he loved her. And even more disturbing was the still-present possibility that she could be pregnant. She forced her elation under control.

"It sounds like you've been very busy while I was in New York."

He swallowed down the lump in his throat and the panic he'd mistakenly thought he'd finally conquered. "There's just one thing that I haven't taken care of yet." He brushed a quick kiss against her lips, as much to give him courage as to fulfill a desire.

He framed his hands around her face and plumbed the depths of her eyes. The love he felt for her nearly overwhelmed him. She meant the world to him. "Jessica...I love you. I love you very much. I'm so sorry that I hurt you, that I wasn't able to say what you wanted to hear. But I can say it now. Nothing has frightened me as much as the thought that I might have lost you for good." He didn't wait for a response to his words.

"I've done everything I can to show you I've made a commitment to the plans I told you about, my desire to give back to the community and help those who've been caught in financial scams. I have no doubts or concerns about my decision to settle permanently in Seattle. It's now time for one last major decision.''

He reached into his pocket. His fingers grazed the velvet box, then passed over it and grabbed a coin. A nervous shiver darted through his body. He held out the coin in the palm of his hand. "This is my lucky coin. I'll make a bet with you. I'll flip the coin. If it lands heads up you'll agree to marry me immediately. If the coin lands tails up...well, what I'll do is clear out of your life and stop disrupting your organized structure.''

A hard jolt of hurt and anger jabbed at every corner of her consciousness. What seconds ago had been overwhelming happiness when he told her he loved her had crashed into the greatest depth of disappointment, pain and anger.

She pulled away from him, grabbing the coin from his hand as she jumped to her feet. Her anger could not keep the underlying hurt from showing up in her voice. "How dare you put the fate of our relationship, of whatever future we might have together, on this—'' she held up the coin, turning it over in her fingers ''—arbitrary toss of a coin! I refuse to stake my future on some whim...on something no more substantial than—''

Her eyes focused on the coin, and her words froze in her throat. It was no ordinary coin. She looked at Dylan as the full implication hit her. It was a two-headed coin. No matter which side landed up, it would show heads. "I—is this a...?''

"If you're trying to ask me if that's a proposal, the answer is yes...that's exactly what it is. I love you. I love you very much. Marry me, Jessica.'' He lowered his mouth to hers with a kiss that spoke of all the love bottled up inside him. If he had been having any last-minute doubts, they had just been dispelled for all time. He pulled her body tighter against his, infusing her with the passion that coursed through his body.

Jessica allowed the kiss to continue for several seconds before breaking the physical connection. *I love you. I love you very much.* His words rang in her ears and echoed in her mind. She felt as if her happiness would burst from her chest. Tears pooled in her eyes, but this time they were tears of joy.

"Oh, Dylan...you don't know how much I've wanted to hear that. I love you, too. I don't know how or when it happened." An almost shy smile tugged at the corners of her mouth. "It might even have started when I was fifteen years old...but I know it's true." Her tears finally overflowed the brims of her eyes and trickled down her cheeks.

He wanted to say something, but an emotional lump caught in his throat and he couldn't get the words out. He kissed the tears away, tasting the saltiness. "I couldn't have done this when you were fifteen years old." He wrapped his arms securely around her. He caressed her shoulders and back, allowing the deep feelings of love to flow through his veins.

"You haven't given me an answer to my proposal yet."

"Are you sure you want to trade in your old life for a commitment of this type? Are you sure you won't find settling down to one place...and *one* woman...a little boring after all your exciting adventures?"

"There's nothing out there that could possibly be more exciting or fulfilling than waking up each morning and knowing that I'll find you next to me and that it will be that way for the rest of our lives. I now know exactly what I want out of life. I want you to marry me. I'll gladly give up who I was in exchange for who I could be—a husband and eventually a father. I want us to be a real family and have a real home.'' He kissed her tenderly on the lips as he pulled her body tightly against his.

''A home and a family…fatherhood,'' she said, easing out of his embrace. She had to tell him, he had to know the possibilities before she could give him an answer.

He looked at her quizzically. ''Is there a problem?''

''Well, there could be. Maybe…I'm not sure.''

Panic darted across his face as he reached out for her, his voice filled with urgency. ''What is it? What's wrong?''

''It's probably nothing. It's just that, uh, the last night we made love at the cabin…well, if you recall, it seems that passion got the better of good sense. We didn't take any precautions.'' She took a calming breath and closed her eyes. ''What I'm trying to say is that there's a possibility I could be pregnant. I'm probably not, but it's possible…''

He threaded his fingers through her hair and cradled her head against his shoulder. ''And if you are, it will only mean that we'll be starting our family a little sooner than we thought. I'll have two people to love rather than just one.''

He reached in his pocket and withdrew the small velvet box. He opened it, took out the diamond ring and placed it on her finger. ''Marry me, Jessica.''

Her hand trembled as she stared at the ring. Her words were a hushed whisper. ''It's beautiful.'' She had never been happier than she was at that moment.

She looked up at him, at the hope that covered his features and the love that glowed in his eyes. "Yes, I'll be honored to marry you."

The immensity of the moment settled over them as they held each other, allowing their love to fill their hearts.

Epilogue

"Jessica?" Dylan stared at the little blue-wrapped bundle cradled in his arms, a look of stark terror on his face. "He's crying."

"Yes, I can hear him." Jessica uttered the words in a calm tone, meant to soothe jangled nerves. She sat in the large rocker holding the tiny pink-wrapped bundle in her arms. "Since he's already been fed, he probably needs a diaper change."

Dylan looked at her, a hopeful expression crossing his face. He took a couple of steps in her direction. "Do you think maybe…"

She looked down at their daughter contentedly nursing, then back at Dylan. "I don't think you're equipped to take over here, but I'm sure you can handle a diaper change without any problems."

"Yes, of course." He set his jaw in a hard line of determination and turned toward the nursery. "I can do this. There won't be any problems. I can handle this.''

Jessica smiled sweetly. ''Of course you can, dear.''

The love she felt for Dylan swelled in her heart as she watched him carry their son into the nursery. She hadn't been sure exactly how he would adjust to instant fatherhood when it was confirmed that she was pregnant, and it had come as quite a shock to both of them when they found out she was carrying twins.

But now she knew. He was going to be a terrific father, just as soon as he got over being frightened of the noisy but helpless little lives they held in their arms. She leaned her head back and closed her eyes, allowing the contented feeling to settle over her.

''He's changed and in bed.''

She opened her eyes and found Dylan kneeling next to her. He placed a tender kiss on her forehead.

''I love you, Mrs. Russell. I love you very much.''

* * * * *

January 2001
TALL, DARK & WESTERN
#1339 by Anne Marie Winston

February 2001
THE WAY TO A RANCHER'S HEART
#1345 by Peggy Moreland

March 2001
MILLIONAIRE HUSBAND
#1352 by Leanne Banks
Million-Dollar Men

April 2001
GABRIEL'S GIFT
#1357 by Cait London
Freedom Valley

May 2001
**THE TEMPTATION OF
RORY MONAHAN**
#1363 by Elizabeth Bevarly

June 2001
A LADY FOR LINCOLN CADE
#1369 by BJ James
Men of Belle Terre

MAN OF THE MONTH

For twenty years Silhouette has been giving
you the ultimate in romantic reads. Come join
the celebration as some of your favorite authors
help celebrate our anniversary with the most
sensual, emotional love stories ever!

Available at your favorite retail outlet.

Where love comes alive™

Don't miss the reprisal of
Silhouette Romance's popular miniseries

**When
King Michael of
Edenbourg goes
missing,**

Royally Wed

The Stanbury Crown

**his devoted
family and loyal
subjects make it
their mission to bring
him home safely!**

Their search begins March 2001 and continues through June 2001.

On sale March 2001: **THE EXPECTANT PRINCESS**
by bestselling author **Stella Bagwell** (SR #1504)

On sale April 2001: **THE BLACKSHEEP PRINCE'S BRIDE**
by rising star **Martha Shields** (SR #1510)

On sale May 2001: **CODE NAME: PRINCE**
by popular author **Valerie Parv** (SR #1516)

On sale June 2001: **AN OFFICER AND A PRINCESS**
by award-winning author **Carla Cassidy** (SR #1522)

Available at your favorite retail outlet.

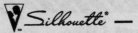
Silhouette —

where love comes alive—online...

eHARLEQUIN.com

shop eHarlequin

- ♥ Find all the new Silhouette releases at everyday great discounts.
- ♥ Try before you buy! Read an excerpt from the latest Silhouette novels.
- ♥ Write an online review and share your thoughts with others.

reading room

- ♥ Read our Internet exclusive daily and weekly online serials, or vote in our interactive novel.
- ♥ Talk to other readers about your favorite novels in our Reading Groups.
- ♥ Take our Choose-a-Book quiz to find the series that matches you!

authors' alcove

- ♥ Find out interesting tidbits and details about your favorite authors' lives, interests and writing habits.
- ♥ Ever dreamed of being an author? Enter our Writing Round Robin. The Winning Chapter will be published online! Or review our writing guidelines for submitting your novel.

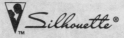